HILLARD HOUSE

It was a pleasure meeting you!

Elizabeth Farris

ELIZABETH FARRIS

outskirts press

Outskirts Press, Inc.
http://www.outskirtspress.com

ISBN: 978-1-9772-1557-4

ACKNOWLEDGEMENTS

I want to thank my friends in Orange Beach, Alabama and Perdido Key, Florida whose support and ideas are invaluable to me. Your special personalities and qualities have helped in developing the characters for this book. You all are always a wealth of information, whether you know it or not.

A special thanks to my good friends Denise McNeely and Angie Snowden whose ideas and thoughts for writing this book were most appreciated. I hope you enjoyed my portrayal of your characters.

CHAPTER ONE

A knock on the door signified that his afternoon siesta was over. He had no idea who would come calling to disrupt his daily routine. All his friends and neighbors knew and respected his two hours of afternoon respite. No texts, no calls and certainly no visits.

Slightly annoyed, he walked to the door and peered out the peak hole. He did not recognize the woman standing on his porch and questioned whether he should open the door. Another knock, slightly harder, made his decision. He swung open the door, the obvious annoyance on his face.

"Hello, Mr. Hillard I presume" the woman said smiling broadly. "My name is Denise McNeely. I'm with McNeely Real Estate Development. Could I have a moment of your time to discuss some options regarding the sale of your property?"

"What makes you think I need options for my property?" was his stern reply.

"Well Mr. Hillard, I happen to hear from

other sources that you might be interested in selling your property? I am very interested in making you an offer. Can you spare a few minutes of your time to hear me out?"

"Look lady, I don't know who your sources are, but I am not in the market to sell this place. And even if I was, it wouldn't be to a Real Estate Developer. Now go away and don't bother me again." With his last remark, he shut the door before she could say another word.

Standing there looking dumbfounded, she couldn't believe her ears. If he had only listened to her pitch, he would have realized that the offer she was ready to make would be far more than what the property was worth. *Stubborn old man. He hasn't heard the last from me.*

Stepping off the porch, she perused the four-acre property. Seated in the driver's seat, she started her BMW 750 and pulled the car around the circular drive and slowly drove down the long driveway that fronted River Road. The front of the property was wooded with minimal landscaping. However, she knew the rear of the property that had over five hundred feet of Intercoastal waterfrontage had been maximized for leisure and entertainment. It was the kind of property she would have liked to own herself.

But she wasn't interested in property for herself. She already had a fabulous home on Ono Island in Orange Beach, Alabama just a few miles away. No, her vision for the property was a ten-story luxury condominium complex with all the bells and whistles that would bring top dollar for each unit.

The land along that stretch of Perdido Key was protected by State Parks and other properties that were not available for the scale of project she was contemplating. She needed the Hillard House to make her dream a reality. She would not be put off so easily. Her wealth and stature in the community was gained by not backing down from a true investment opportunity; and this would be a doosy.

She drove back to her office which took her down along the ocean. She gazed at the many high-rise condos along the coastline and envisioned her own piece of paradise. Her vision did not entail such large-scale buildings that towered high in the sky, but hers would include many other luxuries that those did not. The property along the beach was way over priced which would limit the scope of her plans. That was why she needed the piece of property owned by the Hillard's on the Intercoastal Waterway.

The access from that property to many other bodies of water was tremendous and would add value to each condo she sold. The property and condo amenities that she had envisioned would add additional value and raise the price that she could ask for each condo substantially. It was a golden opportunity that could make her company millions of dollars. Now all she had to do was convince the Hillard's that they needed to sell.

CHAPTER TWO

Sally Hillard had arrived home about thirty minutes after the Real Estate lady had left. Sally was a short woman, blond hair just starting to gray. She was a vibrant woman who loved life and loved her husband even more. Will was waiting for her in the kitchen as she plopped down the groceries she had picked up for a Saturday bash they were hosting. She could see something was off in Will's expression.

"What's the matter Will? You seem to be off somewhere else." Will was the love of her life. She knew every mood, every expression and its meaning. He broke his gaze and looked over at her. Sally knew her husband well. They had been married for over forty years and whenever something bothered him, he didn't have to say a word; *she just knew*.

"There was a Real Estate Developer here today." Sally's eyes widened. "Yeah, she said that someone told her that we were thinking about selling our place." Sally lowered herself to a kitchen chair.

"Who could possibly have told her something like that?" she thought out loud.

"I don't know, but we are not ever going to sell this place to some highfalutin real estate developer so they can tear down our dream home and build some high-dollar condos. No way in hell that'll happen." Will's disgruntled demeanor was so unlike him. He and Sally were great people who enjoyed entertaining their neighbors and had grown very fond of all of them.

Will and Sally had already had this discussion and were in agreement that when their time came, their dream home would remain just as it is now. They had lived there a long time and loved the place. They had purchased it many years prior and had transformed it into their dream home. Neither of them had had much growing up, so when they bought the place, they decided that they would make it into something that they could be proud of; a show place where they could entertain.

They had wanted children, but a physical malady with Sally had resulted in the inability of them bearing children. They were both only children and their parents had died when they were young. They never knew of any relatives even though they had searched to find anyone linked to their past. They were basically two orphans in search of someone. Then they found each other and fell in love. They knew they would be together forever. That's how they survived. But it still left a void where family was concerned. It was difficult to overcome, but they had each other. It was a fact that they would have to deal with. But their love for others was unbounding.

Having no next of kin to leave the place to, they had decided that one of their neighbors whom they had become very fond of would be the recipient of their property. They just hadn't figured out how they would determine who that person would be.

Sure, they could leave it to all of them, but they knew that would cause animosity among themselves before too long. Having too many owners of the property would only cause issues when decisions had to be made. No, it had to be left to only one and all would have to agree that whoever that person turned out to be, there would be no disdain among them.

They loved their home dearly and enjoyed every moment they spent there. They had lived there for the past thirty years and had come to know most of the neighborhood. There was a group of friends that lived in a colorful community next door that had been developed over the last ten years. They became known to the Hillard's as the 'band of nine'. It was a term of endearment, as far as they were concerned.

Bright, colorful two-story homes had been built along the shoreline which added a splash of vibrancy to the area. Over the years, they met and became dear friends with several of them. It was that group alone that would be the pool of potential owners of their estate; they just didn't know it yet.

"Let's not be concerned with some real estate developer. There's nothing they can do to make us sell no matter how much they offer" Sally said to her husband whose concern was still present on his face.

"I know that honey. I was just taken aback by her determination to make us an offer. I don't think we've heard the last of her yet" he said determined to hold his ground. Sally was putting the groceries away when Will walked up behind her and embraced her. "No one will force us to do anything we don't want. And with that, I am going to forget all about Denise McNeely."

Once the groceries were put away, they sat at the kitchen table and discussed the plans for their bash on Saturday. During the summer months, they would entertain their small group of friends at their home. They enjoyed the fun and laughter they could provide for their group of neighbors who they considered family.

Saturday was going to be a small group of close friends starting mid-afternoon with cocktails and a grill out. Once the sun was close to setting, they would all pile into the Hillard's boat and cruise out for a beautiful sunset on the water. The sunsets could be spectacular and coupled with a glass of wine and the gentle sway of the water pushed it over the top.

There was a group of nine that were usually in attendance, the band of nine, and it would be among those nine who would inherit the Hillard House when the time came.

Will and Sally both had had their share of health issues in the past. Will had by-pass surgery a few years back and struggled to keep his blood pressure in check. Sally had a bout of cervical cancer that was eradicated through surgery. But she had been informed that that type of cancer could return elsewhere in her body which left both she and Will concerned. No one knew when their time was up and for that reason alone they felt the need to select the recipient of their inheritance. It would not be an easy task to single one person from the rest, but it was something they knew they needed to do soon.

Two days later the big bash was set to start around 4pm. The forecast promised a beautiful day on tap and Sally was busy in the kitchen preparing hors d'oeuvres and chilling bottles of wine. Will was outside icing a cooler of beer and making sure the grill was ready to fire up once the guests arrived. From all standpoints, everything was in order.

During the past two days, they had discussed how they would select the recipient of their estate. Fairness among the nine candidates was imperative so that there would be no animosity among the close-knit group of friends.

To that end, they decided they would hold a lottery where there would be one lucky winner, but all would have an equal chance. However, they hadn't been able to decide exactly how that lottery would work. They had time to determine how the lottery winner would be selected. One thing they had decided on was that the winner would not be selected until their days were numbered. They agreed that it was the best way to proceed without causing the group any undue anxiety over such unexpected wealth that could be bestowed upon them.

They also agreed that they would inform the group of their plans to hold a lottery during their bash that evening.

CHAPTER THREE

Ever since her visit to the Hillard House, Denise McNeely had been livid over the treatment she received from the old fart who had shunned her away before allowing her to make her pitch. If he thought that was the end of her, he was sorely mistaken. It was not in her nature to give in so easily when such a prize was to be had. No, she had to come up with a strategy to persuade the Hillard's that her offer would be in their best interest.

Denise McNeely had been raised in a poor environment. Her parents had less than nothing, and she vowed that she would not follow in their footsteps. Her father was abusive, and she hated seeing her mother treated like that. She had been abused by him, as well. She refused to allow herself to be treated like her father had treated her mother. She would do better.

When she was old enough, she left the home and took odd jobs to make enough money to take a course in real estate. It was her ticket out of the life she knew as a young girl. She not only strived, she excelled. Her ambition had motivated her to become what she was today.

Her father had long passed away, but she was grateful that her mother had been able to see her little girl rise above the life that she, herself, could never overcome. Denise was able to help her mother financially, but it was all cut short when her mother died of a massive heart attack. She knew that the constant abuse and poverty that her mother lived had played a part in her ailing health. But Denise moved on.

An appointment was scheduled with an old acquaintance of hers whose past was a bit on the shady side. She tried not to associate with her in the public domain for specifically that reason. Denise had spent years building her reputation as a real estate mogul and could not afford to have an unsavory character like Angie Snowden cast a dark shadow on her empire.

Her plan was to meet with Angie to discuss some options available to her in the event that she was unable to persuade the Hillard's to sell their property. Angie could be quite devious, and her skills had come into play on a few prior occasions where actions were required, and major discretion was a must. It was imperative that none of the deeds carried out by Angie Snowden could ever be linked to Denise. That was Angie Snowden's expertise.

Denise's husband, Bruce was not part of her

real estate business and had no idea to what extent his wife would go to be successful. It wasn't that she needed his input, he had his own business that kept him busy traveling on a regular basis. To Denise, that was a blessing in disguise. She didn't think he would approve of some of her past dealings that had risen her to the standing she had now attained. But he was a loyal husband which had kept him from asking any questions that might put her under scrutiny.

Angie Snowden lived in Pensacola Beach, Florida which was only twenty miles away from Denise's office in Orange Beach, Alabama. They agreed to meet on Monday at a small restaurant on Gulf Breeze Island which was a tourist destination that allowed for anonymity. Bruce McNeely would be out of town that day which allowed Denise to keep her meeting a secret from him. Bruce knew of Angie vaguely but had no idea what she did for a living or the depths she would go for a good price. That tidbit of information would remain unknown as well as Denise's communications with her should there be any fallout from Angie's actions, whatever they might be.

Denise had tried to call the Hillard's several times over the past couple days and each time they answered and realized what the call was about, they hung up on her. The more they dismissed her, the more determined Denise became. This would be the project that would put her career and stature in the real estate world over the top.

It was unfathomable why that stupid old couple would refuse to deal with her. Why did they care if a luxury condominium complex was built on their property? The money they would receive for their land would persuade almost anyone to sell. Why were they being so stubborn?

Denise already knew the Hillard's had no family left to leave the property to. So why would they care what happened to the place once they were dead and gone? It made no sense. But they had to have a reason and that was where Angie Snowden would come in. Angie had a way of finding out information that even the best investigators couldn't find. The tactics she used would not be of consequence to Denise as long as she delivered the information on why the Hillard's would want to hold on to their property when there was no living heir to leave it to. That task would be assigned to Angie during their lunch meeting on Monday.

Promptly at 1pm, Angie Snowden walked into the Bridge Bar and Sunset Grill just across the Pensacola Bay Bridge. Denise was sitting in a corner booth that looked out over the water. There was just a sprinkling of patrons which was unusual for that time of day, but Denise was glad for the privacy.

Angie slid in the booth seat across from Denise and shook her hand.

"I was surprised to hear from you Denise. It's been a while since we last spoke" Angie said smiling as she knew there would be a nice pay-day in her near future.

"It's good to see you Angie. You're looking well."

"Thanks" Angie responded carefully watching Denise's demeanor. "So, I'm assuming you have a job for me?"

"As a matter of fact, I would like to hire you to find out some information on a couple who are unwilling to sell their property to me."

The waitress came over and took their lunch order, then once she was gone, Denise explained the nature of their business. She explained in depth everything she already knew about the Hillard's and her attempts to present them with a very lucrative offer to no avail. She gave some detail on her plans for the property and why it was imperative for her to purchase the four acres of prime real estate where the Hillard's house was situated.

Angie was slightly surprised that their business hadn't been more of a scandalous nature which was usually why her skills were required. But the pay was good, and she agreed to find out just why the Hillard's were so reluctant to sell. She told Denise that it might take a couple weeks but that she would find out the reason and con-tact her as soon as she had the information.

The rest of their lunch was spent on small talk with an agreement to talk again soon. Denise paid the check and shook Angie's hand then turned to leave. Walking to her car, she breathed a sigh of relief knowing that Angie would get the information she needed. Once she had that, she could adjust her strategy to get the Hillard property on her books. She drove back to Orange Beach knowing that she would do whatever it took to make her dream project come to fruition. No holds barred.

CHAPTER FOUR

Music filled the air and a gentle breeze made for a very pleasant day to throw a party. The Hillard's had invited their close-knit group of friends for an evening of food and festivities. They had done this on many occasions before. But this evening would be different. They would inform their good friends that one of them would inherit the property once the Hillard's were gone.

Their friends had no idea just how soon that could happen. Sure, they knew of Will's medical procedures. But no one knew just how bad the elder Hillard's were. That news would not be revealed until the end of the evening so that there would not be a cloud hanging over the group during the party.

Will and Sally Hillard were a lively couple who enjoyed entertaining. They relished in the presence of friends. They had no children which had devastated the young couple, at the time, when they were informed on Sally's inability to bear children. They had thought about adoption but couldn't bear the thought that some young mother would have a change of heart and take the child back. They were not willing to take that risk. But they had built a wonderful, happy life together and any regrets they previously had, were gone now. They were old now but never looked back on what could have been.

It was five o'clock and the guests would soon be arriving. Everything was ready. It would be an evening to remember as were all their parties. Sally and Will were sitting outside when the first of their guests arrived.

"Well hello. Come join us" said Sally standing to greet two of their good friends, Angie and Sean Callen. "We're so glad you could make it."

"You know we would never miss one of your parties Sally" Angie said giving her a hug. Will had just reached the couple and shook Sean's hand then hugged Angie.

"What would you like to drink?" asked Will to his young guests. Angie and Sean had been married for four years and had moved into the neighborhood a year before. They had gotten to know Sally and Will almost immediately thanks to another friend of the Hillard's.

Angie was a beautiful girl with big eyes and shoulder length blond hair. She was slender with a bubbly personality that could put a smile on anyone's face. Both Sean and Angie were in their early thirties. Sean was dark haired and quite attractive himself. They made an adorable couple and Sally and Will looked upon them as family.

"I'll have a beer and Angie will have her usual white wine" replied Sean. By the time the drinks were served, another of the invited guests arrived. David Flaherty was a widower whose wife had died suddenly at a young age. He lived alone in the home he and his wife shared prior to her death. David was a retired Captain in the Navy. He was tall and handsome but since his wife's death two years ago, there was no other woman who had yet to capture his heart.

"Hey everyone, great day for a party" he said as he pulled a beer from the cooler. Sally rushed to him and hugged him. She had been the one who nurtured and consoled him during his rough days just after he lost his wife.

Ginger and Thomas Irick were next to arrive. The crowd was growing quickly and soon all invitees would be present. Thomas was a resident at the Banana Bay community as were all the other guests. The small community was adjacent to the Hillard's property. Both shared a stretch of beach on the Intercoastal Waterway which was how they all became such good friends. Ginger had met Thomas nearly a year earlier and quickly became part of the close-knit group of friends.

Lyle Stephens and Joshua Wade arrived together. Both men were divorced and had become close buddies ever since. Both divorces had been rough on the men but neither had children which in hindsight, was considered a blessing, knowing the outcome.

Sally had never really taken to Lyle's wife Tracey and was often vocal about her feelings. Tracey could be quite brash at times and often criticized Lyle in public which Sally found inappropriate. When Lyle found out about Tracey's infidelity, he divorced her and sent her packing.

Josh's wife of three years was quiet and often chose not to associate with the rest of the group. She often kept to herself and wanted Josh to stay with her constantly. The two finally drifted apart and had an amicable divorce. Josh's wife moved back to Louisiana where she was originally from. It saddened Sally and Will to see the marriage fall apart but had been a pillar of support whenever Josh needed it.

The last to arrive was Frank Barber and his pretty wife Phyllis. They had met the Hillard's shortly after they were married twenty years prior and had moved into the Banana Bay Beach Community from California. Over the years, the group of nine had become as close to being family with the Hillard's as could be. They all partied together, had dinner at each other houses and just enjoyed each other's company as often as possible. But Sally and Will were the eldest of the group and looked upon the group of nine as their children; something that had been lacking for them their entire life.

The party was in full swing now that all attendees were present. The grill was fired up, the drinks were flowing, and music filled the air. Several boaters passed by and waved. When the steaks were ready, everyone gathered at the two picnic tables. There was an abundance of food that was passed around till everyone had a plate full.

Sally and Will looked over their friends and took such pleasure in being a part of each of their lives. They had been blessed to have found each one of them.

Once everyone had finished eating, they all pitched in and cleared the tables to make ready for the sunset cruise that was always a highlight at the Hillard parties. While the girls helped Sally clean up the dishes, the guys all helped in loading the boat with drinks for the cruise.

Will had an older boat that had served them well over the years. Being such a stickler for perfection, Will had kept his boat in pristine condition. The inside cabin was spacious as well as the open upper deck that offered great views of the sunset. Once everyone was aboard, they shoved off in the direction of Wolf Bay that would avail them spectacular sunset vistas. Once there, Sally and Will would inform the group of the plans for their estate.

The sun was just beginning to set. The bright oranges and reds set the sky ablaze. It was breathtaking. Everyone sat in silence as the sun slowly began to dip below the horizon. The lower it got, the more brilliant the colors. It seemed like only moments before the sun was just a peak of orange and then was gone. The colors still radiated the sky when Will stood up amongst the group and stated that he and Sally had an announcement to make.

Everyone looked around at each other bewildered.

"Now, don't look so confused" Will said smiling. "Sally and I have been wanting to tell you all about a decision that we have recently agreed upon. You all know that we don't have any living relatives and that you all are as close to family as we have. You also know that Sally and I are getting up in years and both of us have health issues. What we want to do is, when the time comes for us to pass on, we want someone to inherit our estate and keep this tradition alive."

Immediately the group threw out remarks saying that they weren't going anywhere anytime soon and that it was nonsense to talk like that. But Sally held up a hand and stood next to her husband.

"We love all of you dearly and think of you as our family. Since we have no one to leave our property to, we want to select one of you to be the recipient. Since we cannot choose one of you specifically, we plan to do it as a sort of lottery. A random selection because we cannot choose just one of you."

"Why don't you divide it up equally between all of us? That way you wouldn't have to choose" Lyle said. Will responded.

"We discussed that too, but we were afraid that if the property was owned by all of you and there were decisions to be made that everyone had to agree upon, it could cause a rift between some of you and we do not want that to happen."

"We know how close all of you are and what good friends you have all become over the years. We know that whoever inherits this place, it will be accepted by all of you. We do not want to sell this place to a developer. We want it to stay just the way it is and that what we have enjoyed over the years will continue once we're gone. Can you all agree with our wishes? And if anyone does not want to be included in this lottery, per se, is free to opt out. We are just adamant that who-ever received the property will not sell it to a developer. That is an absolute insistence, and everyone must agree to that."

The group remained silent trying to grasp the magnitude of what they were just told. Will started the engine and began the cruise back home. "I want you all to consider what we told you tonight and take all the time you need to

think about it. We're not planning on check-
ing out anytime soon. We just wanted to let you
know what we were planning to do. So, with that
being said, when we get back, I want everyone
to continue the party and let's enjoy our time together. All in favor!"

"Here, here" was the yell back from the group
and so the festivities continued.

Will and Sally were pleased that their
friends were receptive to their plan. They so
wanted the group to carry on after they could
not. It was a tradition that they had built over
a long period of time and hated to think that
it would end. They now had reassurance that
the legacy would continue. The thought of their
friends enjoying the home they had loved for so
long made them smile.

The party continued till well after midnight.
There was a certain joy in the air which made
the evening even more special. They could rest
easy now.

CHAPTER FIVE

Denise McNeely paced back and forth across her office. She had called Angie Snowden three times wanting an update regarding the Hillard property. It had been a week since she met with Angie and she wanted answers. Finally, her phone rang. It was Angie.

"It's about time Angie, I've called three times. What have you found out?"

"Sorry Denise, but I wasn't able to answer when you called. I do have some news though and you're not going to like it."

"What is it?" Denise asked

"It seems that Mr. and Mrs. Hillard are planning on giving their estate to one lucky friend of theirs." Denise's mouth dropped.

"What in the hell does that mean. Who just gives away a gold mine like that?"

"Well, I got this from a friend of mine who knows one of the potential recipients. She said that the Hillard's had a party Saturday night for a group of close friends and announced that one of them would inherit the estate. It was going to be done by some kind of random drawing. But the worst part is that one of the stipulations of the recipient is that it could never be sold to a developer."

"Son of a bitch. I can't allow that to happen. I need them to sell to me no matter what it takes to persuade them. Do you have any ideas on what I can do to persuade them Angie?" Denise knew that Angie had no qualms about getting a little rough with folks who needed assistance in seeing it her way. But Denise did not want anything to lead back to her. Angie was quiet for a moment.

"I'm not sure how far you'd like me to go, but I'm sure I can come up with some ideas to aide in the persuasion. Do you want to know the details?"

"No details please. The less I know about it, the better. I'll trust your judgement on the course of action. Do you have a price in mind?" Denise had a large budget if Angie could pull it off.

"I don't have a number in mind yet. It will all be based on what actions I have to take and how much risk is involved. If I pull it off for you, I know it will be worth every penny of my fee."

"OK Angie. Do what you have to and keep me posted of your progress. Just no details and only burner phones." Denise had no idea what Angie had instore for the Hillard's, but one thing was for sure, Angie would get the job done. With a swell of relief, she hung up the phone and would start the waiting game. In the meantime, she would refine her plans for the project and have everything ready when the time came to make the purchase.

Angie looked over her list of recipients of the coveted Hillard house. There was a total of nine potential winners. The Barber's, Irick's and the Callen's were all married couples. The three remaining, Lyle Stephenson, Joshua Wade and David Flaherty, were single men. She wasn't sure what her plans would entail or how far she would go to persuade these individuals to opt-out of the agreement, but she had some ideas.

Denise's husband had no idea that his wife had hired the services of Angie Snowden and would likely disapprove had he known. He was aware of other dealings Denise had with Angie and had made his opinion apparent. He knew his wife could be a ruthless negotiator, but he didn't like the element of darkness that came with Angie Snowden.

Denise had decided to keep her agreement with Angie to herself. No need to get Bruce stressed over the whole ordeal. He knew that Denise was wanting to purchase the Hillard property, but the rest of the details had been vague. All the better, as far as he was concerned. He had his own business to tend to and it had its own set of issues. His wife was capable of handling her own dilemmas.

CHAPTER SIX

Saturday's weather was promising to be a beautiful day for a boat ride. Thomas and Ginger Irick rarely took out the speed boat because of its tremendous horsepower. Most of the time the boat was stored at the Sportsman Marina which housed hundreds of huge boats for a handsome fee. Thomas and Ginger had no issues paying the price to keep their boat secure.

Thomas Irick was a successful collector and reseller of antique cars that had proved to be a very lucrative business. He had built substantial wealth over the past ten years. A year and a half prior, he had met his wife Ginger. She had caught his eye at an auction and had asked her out. They married just six months later and had become inseparable ever since.

They had plans to go boating on Saturday as they had on many days. But instead of taking out one of the many boats available to them through the Freedom Club, they wanted to take their precious *My Lady*. The Baha cigarette boat by that name was a beauty. Long and sleek, it was white with a wide yellow stripe that ran the length of the boat. It had the power of a small jet engine. They loved gliding over the water at speeds that would make your head spin. When Thomas and Ginger's boat passed by, heads turned.

They spent a few hours on Friday at the Cobalt Restaurant; one of their favorite hangouts. Cobalt was a local destination that catered to the many tourists that visited Orange Beach, Alabama. Many of their friends showed up there on a regular basis and they all loved the proximity the restaurant had with the Perdido Pass. The Pass was the only access to the Gulf of Mexico in that area. All the fishing charter boats and luxury pleasure boats floated through the Pass directly in view of the Cobalt outside patio.

Early Saturday arrived just as promised and the day was heating up quickly. After breakfast, they packed some lunch and drinks to take along on the boat ride. They planned on going out on the gulf since the water was reported very calm.

They might even go all the way to Destin if they so wished. Once the cooler was packed and all necessities for a day on the water were gathered, they drove to the Sportsman where the boat was already in the water and awaiting their arrival. They packed the boat with the coolers and climbed aboard.

They eased out of the slip where their boat had been prepped before their arrival. Gassed and ready to go was one of the perks of the fee they paid. It was well worth it. They followed the no-wake signs until they cleared the marina. They maneuvered the boat over to the deep channel that passed by the Caribe, a three-building high-rise luxury condominium complex.

The waterway leading out to the Perdido Pass was shallow and they took caution to stay in the deep channel until they were out on the open sea. So many boats were doing the same. Fishing boats anchored under the Perdido Pass bridge catching bait fish for their charter runs. Others were just out for a day on the ocean. Many other small craft stayed inside the Pass and beached themselves on the many islands throughout the bays and rivers that funneled toward the Pass.

It was just a beautiful day for boating. Once out on the ocean, Thomas kicked up the throttle and quickly the massive speed boat raised its bow out of the water, planed off, then flew across the sea as if it was gliding on air. The wind was warm on their faces as they cruised along parallel with the beach. Thomas liked to gun the engines occasionally just to feel the pure power at his command. He would back it down for the long cruise they had planned for the day.

Heading East a few hundred yards offshore, the beach goers were barely visible. A couple sitting in beach chairs along the water's edge watched as the bright yellow speed boat skipped across the water. One could only imagine the feeling of being engulfed by so much power. You didn't see many cigarette boats cruising the ocean, but when you did, they were a spectacular sight.

Just as the boat was passing to the east of them, they heard a huge explosion followed by a ball of fire where the boat had just been. Jumping to their feet, it was obvious that the white and yellow speed boat and blown up and was ablaze just off the coastline. They called 911 and reported what they saw.

Other boats that had been in the area sped toward the scene, but the fire was so big that they couldn't get very close. Searching the water around the explosion area looking for survivors, it was evident that no one could have survived such a blast. It was unknown how many were on-board or who the boat belonged too, but that revelation would soon be made.

CHAPTER SEVEN

T he coast guard was quickly on the scene and attempts to put out the fire were underway. Emergency vehicles had also collected along the beach and were awaiting information on rescue efforts. It wouldn't take long before identification of the boaters was made. There was some speculation on who owned the boat and the boat license number had confirmed the owner. It would take forensics to determine if it was the owners themselves who had occupied the boat that day.

The Medical Examiner was on scene when the bodies of the victims were retrieved from the water. The bodies were unrecognizable. The magnitude of the blast had wreaked massive damage to the face, torso and limbs of the victims. The scene on the beach was gruesome.

On lookers had stated that there were only two people on board, as much as they could tell. Both bodies were eventually turned over to the ME. The extensive damage to the victims was a sign of how powerful the blast was.

Coast Guard had run the license number which showed the current owners to be Thomas and Ginger Irick. The manager at the Sportsman Marina had stated that the Irick's had taken the boat out earlier that day. Within twenty-four hours, DNA would also confirm that the occupants were in-deed Thomas and Ginger Irick.

All the news channels were flashing their 'Breaking News' ticker announcing the terrible boat explosion that had happened just off the shore of Orange Beach, Alabama. There hadn't been an accident like that in decades. Some video of the explosion had been captured on a couple condominium complexes and had been turned over to investigators.

News cameras had been viewing the salvage effort of what was remaining of the high-dollar Baha cigarette boat. The reports stated that the initial inspection showed a massive explosion, but the cause was not yet determined.

One camera angle had caught footage of the boat approaching from the west. There was no visible sign of smoke from the engine compartment or any other evidence that the boat was in distress. It looked as though the boat just blew up. It was a strange scenario, but that didn't mean there wasn't something wrong that was not visible. The forensic team would determine the cause of the explosion. Once that information was obtained, it could be ruled an accident or possibly something more sinister.

A coast guard salvage vessel was able to retrieve several parts of the wreckage and were bringing them ashore to be transported to the forensic lab. Even more disturbing was the discovery of a foot that had been blown off one of the victim's bodies; presumably the female victim. The outboard engines were also retrieved and appeared to be intact. They would be crucial in determining the cause of the blast. The salvage operations lasted for hours while local law enforcement canvased the beach area for witnesses to take their statements.

Word spread fast throughout the community of the tragic accident. It hadn't been broadcast who the victims were pending next of kin notification, but footage of the explosion had gone viral as well as the footage of the big white and yellow boat just prior to the blast. Not many people owned a boat like that so there was someone who knew the owners and could surmise that the victims had been friends of theirs.

By nightfall, everything that could be salvage had been floated to shore and off-loaded to a waiting transport vehicle. The huge crowd that had filled the beach earlier, had dissipated. All local law personnel had left the scene. Just a lingering smell of smoke was the only sign that a disaster had recently occurred there.

It would now be up to the professionals to determine exactly what had caused the horrific blast that had claimed two lives. The work was just beginning. Next of kin would be made which left friends and family devastated that their good friends were killed by some tragic accident. It was so unfair. They were so young to be taken so soon was the sentiment.

CHAPTER EIGHT

The small, close-knit group of friends gathered at the Hillard's house once the news broke of the identities of the two boat victims. They had already known who it was from the footage of the boat that aired earlier on TV. But the verbalization of the names of the victims had hit them all hard. The realization that two of their dear friends had just died in a terrible accident was devastating. All they could do now was mourn the death of their friends and support each other through their own grief.

"I just don't see how this could have happened" Sally said as the tears streamed down her face. Will put his arm around her shoulder but there was just no comfort that could be found.

"You know, Thomas always kept that boat in perfect shape. It just makes no sense" Josh said pacing the floor. They all shook their heads in agreement. Will turned to the group.

"We all knew and loved Thomas and Ginger and it's just so hard to believe that they're gone.

It was a tragedy that has no rational explanation. I think the only thing left to do is wait to hear the results of the investigation. There's no doubt in my mind that the authorities will get to the bottom of what caused that boat to blow up."

It was a somber gathering which was not the norm. When they were all together, there was nothing but laughter and happiness among them. They wondered if it would ever be the same now that two of their flock would no longer be among them.

The night grew late, but no one wanted to leave the company of their friends. Eventually, one by one they departed. Hugs abounded as each of them knew the sense of loss they would feel for so long.

Thomas and Ginger's parents had been notified and were on their way to identify their children. The ME had done her best to make the two victims presentable, considering the extensive damage that had been done to the bodies. Their upper torsos had sustained much the same amount of damage as the lower. Their faces were badly burned but they were easily recognized by their parents.

However, they could not be spared the extreme grief of seeing their child lying lifeless on that metal table covered by a sheet. The pain and suffering at that moment would never go away.

Once both families had left, the ME prepared

the bodies for autopsy. There would be a story to be told from their remains in hopes of determining that this was just some terrible accident. The evidence doesn't lie.

The forensics team had worked around the clock examining every item that was recovered from the water. The experts were scouring over even the most minute objects to understand what happened. Everyone involved had to have an open mind, but each was hoping that their investigation would result in a finding of a faulty engine. No one wanted to imagine that the explosion could have been done on purpose. If that ended up being the case, it was a whole new ball game. Time and attention to detail along with forensic analysis would tell the tale.

The following day, the FBI had been informed that the cause of the explosion had been a bomb that was planted on the boat and triggered by a cell phone detonator. The news of that revelation had reporters running rampant for a story.

Shock and dismay filled the airwaves. No one could have imagined that the horrific boat explosion that killed two local residents had been done on purpose. The news hit the community very hard. People walked around town in disbelief. Who could have done such a terrible deed?

Those who had known and loved the Irick's were left to deal with the fact that someone had murdered Thomas and Ginger. It was just one more harrowing detail they would have to cope with.

CHAPTER NINE

The FBI had arrived on scene shortly after being notified that a bomb had been the cause of the boat explosion that killed two locals. The media circus that ensued had been relentless in their attempts at getting the details before any other reporter. It was a disgrace to see the media scrambling for information in order to scoop their competition. Where was their sympathy for the actual victims?

FBI Special Agent James Townsend had been assigned to the case and was being briefed by the local law enforcement. Once up to speed, Townsend had assembled his crew to take the lead in the investigation.

Townsend had been with the FBI for years and was one of their top agents. He was tall, standing around six foot three, muscular in build from many hours in the gym. His wavy light brown hair and strong cheek bones made him very easy on the eyes. But when it came to murder, he could be as hard as a rock in seeking the truth.

After reading over the reports and interviews that had already been collected, he wanted to revisit the scene and speak with the witnesses himself. He also wanted to talk with the friends and family who knew the victims the best. Since this was ruled a homicide, he needed to find out just who would want Thomas and Ginger Irick dead; if they were, indeed, the actual target.

"Agent Collins, you come with me" Townsend said looking over at Jack Collins. With a nod, Collins and Townsend left headquarters for the crime scene.

Agent Jack Collins was a seasoned veteran with the FBI and was part of the local unit based in Pensacola, Florida. He lived in the area and knew it well. Before joining the FBI, Collins was a cop for the Perdido Police force for ten years. He knew of Thomas and Ginger Irick and would be a valuable asset in helping determine who and where to look for information.

Their first stop was at the beach area where the witnesses had watched the explosion occur. He wanted a feel for the distance between the shoreline and where the actual blast zone was. After about fifteen minutes, they decided to speak with the parents. It wouldn't be a pleasant conversation, but one that needed to take place. It was known that Thomas and Ginger lived in a small community of colorful homes on River Road called Banana Bay Beach Resort

Community. They would need to talk to each one of them individually. If anyone knew of some adversity in the Irick's life, it would be them.

Frank Barber and his wife Phyllis were home when Townsend knocked on their door. Before saying anything, Townsend and Collins both flashed their badges.

"Mr. Barber?" Townsend asked. Frank nodded. "I'm FBI Special Agent Townsend and this is Agent Collins. We're here regarding the boat accident that killed Thomas and Ginger Irick. Can we have a few minutes of your time?" Frank opened the door wide and nodded.

"Sure, come on in." As the two agents entered the Barber home, Frank motioned them to have a seat in the living room. The room was spacious and nicely decorated.

"Since Thomas and Ginger live nearby, we were hoping you might be able to give us some information about them. Did you know them very well?" Townsend asked taking out his notepad.

"Yeah we did. We're actually pretty good friends and have been for around four years. As soon as I saw the footage of the boat that exploded, I knew it was them" Frank said lowering his head. His wife Phyllis was already tearing up as Frank tried to comfort her. Frank continued. "You see, we've been on that boat with Thomas and Ginger before on several occasions.

The paint job on Thomas's boat is very distinct. I've never seen another boat around here like it. That's how I knew it had to be his."

"I understand" Townsend said, then continued. "We have also been informed that the boat had been sabotaged. By that, I mean a bomb had been placed on their boat at some point and then detonated." The expressions on the Barber's faces was that of shock. "Do you know of anyone that might want to hurt the Irick's?"

"No, no one at all. Everyone that we ever associated with had only spoke highly of them" Frank responded.

"Do you know of anyone else that would have access to their boat?" Townsend asked. Phyllis sat on the couch with her head in her hands trying to hold back her tears. She was totally distraught, so Frank did his best to answer their questions.

"I know that Thomas always kept his boat in top shape. He used to keep it at his house but decided to store it at the Sportsman a couple years ago. He said it was much easier to pay to have it stored than it was to haul it to the boat launch when he wanted to take it out. I think the Sportsman Marina is pretty secure, but I really couldn't know. I don't know of anyone that had ever used his boat without Thomas manning the helm. He was very particular about that."

"Well, if you think of anything else that

might be useful, please call me" Townsend said handing Frank his card. Both agents rose and offered their condolences, shook hands with Frank and left. Frank walked them to the door then returned to console his wife.

Back in the car Collins suggested going straight to the Sportsman to see just how secure their storage facility is. They arrived at the Sportsman and were escorted to the manager's office. The manager's name was Eric Meyer. After making the introductions, Eric had them sit opposite him and proceeded to tell them how upset he was that such a thing could happen. He said he knew the Irick's well since they used the facilities to not only store the cigarette boat, but they also belonged to the Freedom Club which loans out boats to members for a reasonable price.

Townsend and Collins both asked questions regarding the security of the boats in storage and who had access to them at any given time. They were given a list of employees that would have access. Townsend responded.

"Is it possible for someone to gain access to one of the boats without anyone noticing? I'm asking because someone placed a bomb on the Irick's boat sometime prior to them taking it out. So, at some point, someone got to their boat and was able to plant the bomb and leave the marina, all undetected. Can you tell me how something like that could happen Mr. Meyer?" Eric Meyer's face turned flush as he tried to answer their question.

"Look, it's not impossible for someone to gain access to the marina late at night. We have never had anything like this happen before. Not even someone vandalizing a boat or trying to steal one. Our record has been stellar in that regard. If someone planted the bomb on the Irick's boat, I guess it's possible for someone to find a way to accomplish it. I just can't understand why they would want to kill someone in such a manner."

Townsend and Collins were shown where the Irick's boat had been stored. During the off-season, Meyer said that the boat would have been stored inside on the second level. But at present, the boat was stored on ground level of a three-tiered rack. It wouldn't take a genius to be able to get to the boat while it was stored outside. That left a plethora of potential suspects. They would need to narrow it down. Someone wanted the Irick's dead.

CHAPTER TEN

The funeral for the Irick's came and went with many friends and family attending. The double funeral was held at a small church in Perdido Key not far from where the Irick's lived. The outpouring of grief was immense. The parents of Thomas and Ginger were hard to watch. The deaths of their children had left them pale and weak even though they were only in their fifties.

The service had ended early in the afternoon and the crowd was slowly departing. It left many wondering who could hurt such good people. They had no clue what the answer to that question could be.

A couple weeks passed with no new leads on who wanted the Irick's dead. Townsend and Collins had interviewed the employees at the Sportsman Marina along with the rest of the neighbors who knew the Irick's. No one provided any information that could point them in a direction of a suspect. No motive could be established but that would not deter Townsend and Collins.

It wasn't as if Townsend hadn't had tough cases before, but the victims in this case was perplexing. The manner in which they were murdered was not ordinary either. But Townsend had been able to solve cases that had little to go on before. He would not stop until he brought justice to the family and friends of Thomas and Ginger Irick.

Gradually, the community moved on. It served no purpose to dwell on something they could not solve. Grief could take a lot out of people if they allow it to rule their lives. The Hillard's decided to have a party to celebrate the lives of Thomas and Ginger Irick in hopes of keeping their memory alive and helping their friends to move on.

All were in agreement that it would be a tribute to their friends who would want them to continue to enjoy life even though they were gone. The party would be the following Saturday. Just like always with a grill out and sunset cruise.

When Saturday arrived, it was difficult to get into the party mode knowing that two of their dear friends would not be in attendance. In fact, the party was in their honor which made their grief heighten as if it had just happened yesterday. It would be a struggle to carry on without them but with the help of the Hillard's and the others, they would manage.

Sally and Will had set up the outside just

the way they always had. Music was playing
when the guests began arriving. It was a sullen
moment as each of them entered the Hillard's
house, but eventually, they all let go of their
grief and toasted their fallen friends. Happy stories were told and as the sun began to go down,
they all boarded the Hillard's boat and set out
on the Intercoastal to watch the sun set. It was a
glorious sunset but in the background of everyone's mind was a sadness that their friends were
no longer there to enjoy it.

The party went on well past midnight and
by the time everyone had left, Will and Sally felt
as though they had done their best to build the
spirits of not only themselves, but their remaining group of friends.

Two more weeks passed, and everyone was
moving on with their lives. The FBI's investigation had stalled. There were just no leads as to
who would want the Irick's dead. The boat and
bomb had been so damaged that no evidence
could be found to link a suspect to the crime. It
seemed that the murders would not be solved.
Something had to give.

It was a beautiful morning and as he did
most mornings, Lyle Stephenson had prepared
to take his ten-mile bike ride before the heat of
the day set in. At 8am, Lyle rolled his bike out
of the garage, put on his helmet and began his
ride that would take him down River Road to

Perdido Key Drive, a scenic highway that ran along the coastline. From there he would go East a few miles to the base of the bridge that spanned the Intercoastal Waterway and back around to River Road and home.

He always took the same route because it was loaded with scenic views of the ocean and Intercoastal. He made his way out of the complex and turned right onto River Road. The air was fresh and clean, and the smell of the sea lingered in the air. There was very little traffic on River Road at that time of day. He was cruising along when he heard the sound of an approaching vehicle in the distance behind him. He moved over to the right and stayed in the designated bike path.

Looking over his shoulder he could see a dark pick-up truck approaching about a quarter mile behind. It was approaching fast, so he moved even further to the right to allow it to pass. As the truck was within thirty feet of him, he heard the truck accelerate. In seconds it was directly behind him. The truck plowed into Lyle before he could react catapulting his body into the air and landing fifty feet ahead onto the pavement. The bike was a tangled mess as Lyle lay there dead on impact. The truck slowed as it passed Lyle's broken body then sped off. No other cars had been on the road. Finally, a local resident that lived along River Road was heading out to run some errands and spotted Lyle's body and called 911.

Emergency vehicles arrived quickly, but Lyle was pronounced dead at the scene. It didn't take investigators long to determine that Lyle had been the victim of a hit and run. It didn't take long before the news was carrying the breaking story. Another one of the band of nine was dead.

CHAPTER ELEVEN

A gents Townsend and Collins had heard the reports of the hit and run that killed Lyle Stephenson. There was no reason to assume the two cases were linked, but something in Townsend's gut told him that something was odd about the cases. He found it strange that another one of the close-knit group of friends was also killed. Was it just a coincidence that three members of the Hillard's friends had been murdered in the span of just a few weeks? He didn't think so. What was it about this group of people that seemed to have put a target on their backs?

Lyle's mother was notified by the local police department. She lived in nearby Pensacola. The news had devastated the woman who could barely talk to Agent Townsend and Collins. She could think of no-one that would want her son dead.

They contacted Lyle's ex-wife but found no reason to suspect she had anything to do with the hit and run. They would need to question everyone who knew Lyle to determine if there was a link between the two incidents.

It was possible that it was just a random hit and run with no connection to the Irick's murder, but it just didn't jive for Townsend. Three friends all murdered in such a short span of time couldn't be a coincidence. There was something there and Townsend knew he had to find out what before someone else paid with their life.

Sally and Will Hillard had been at home when they heard the news. They were inconsolable. Agents Townsend and Collins were, once again, at the Hillard's to collect any information that could help in identifying who could be behind the murders of three of their friends.

The Hillard's had informed the agents that Lyle was a creature of habit. They stated that Lyle almost always took a bike ride in the morning, sometimes even when it was raining. They had witnessed cars speeding down River Road on several occasions, but the bike lane was wide enough for cars to pass without coming close to the cyclist. They said that Lyle was always very cautious when he was out riding his bike. He was always careful when cars were approaching and that he had been riding that ten-mile course for years with no incidents.

"Someone would have had to veer over into the bike lane in order to run Lyle down" Will Hillard had told the agents. "This was no accident where someone hit Lyle and left the scene. This was murder." Sally could do nothing but sob into her husband's shoulder.

The agents gave their condolences to the Hillard's for the second time in as many months then left them to their grief. They would need to make the same rounds as they did with the Irick murders. They just couldn't understand why someone would want to kill these people.

The next stop would be at Angie and Sean Callen's home. They lived only four houses away from Lyle and hoped that they could shed some light on who might want Lyle Stephenson dead. They knocked on the door of the brightly painted house. All the houses in the Banana Bay Beach community were painted in vivid colors. The Callen's home was a two story, royal blue house that sat one row back from the small sandy beach that fronted the Intercoastal Waterway.

Sean answered the door and wasn't surprised to see the same two agents that had questioned them not so long ago about the Irick's. He didn't say a word, just opened the door for them to come inside.

Angie was sitting on the sofa. Her eyes were red and puffy from crying as she sat with her hands in her lap, her head down. She looked up as the men entered the living room. Her expression was dire. She was a very attractive woman in her early thirties. Even through the tears, you could see her stunning beauty. It was a shame that such a pretty face should be covered in despair.

"How can we help you gentlemen?" Sean asked motioning for them to have a seat. Townsend told them how Lyle's murder looked to have been intentional; not some random hit and run. They were stunned by the thought that someone had also targeted Lyle. Angie looked up.

"But why?" she asked.

"We were hoping that maybe you might have some idea as to why someone could have targeted three of your friends." Collins knew the Callen's vaguely and felt a pang of sadness for their loss of another good friend.

"Is there anything that has happened in the last few months that might put your friends in jeopardy?" Townsend asked. Both Angie and Sean looked at each other puzzled. Then suddenly Sean's eyes widened as he looked back at the agents.

"There is one thing new that we were made aware of about three months ago that involved both the Irick's and Lyle" Sean said then continued. "Our friends, the Hillard's, had all of us over for a party one Saturday night and told us that they were planning on leaving their estate to one of us. The estate is worth easily a million dollars and the recipient would be determined by some kind of lottery that they would have.

One of nine of us would inherit the place and we all had to agree that we wouldn't sell the property. They said if any of us didn't want to be part of it, that would be our choice. We all agreed to participate. But I don't see how that would fit into some kind of murder scheme. There is not one of us nine that would ever hurt another. We are very good friends and have been for some time."

The story sounded very intriguing and would warrant further investigation. If this so-called lottery was behind the murders of the Irick's and Lyle Stephenson, that would leave the remaining six friends as suspects.

After leaving the Callen residence, Townsend and Collins went to interview the remaining four lottery participants to see if any of them was hiding something. One couple, Phyllis and Frank Barber were older and didn't come off to be murderers. Of course, Sean and Angie Callen had been the one's to tell them about the lottery and also didn't seem like they could have committed the three murders. That left Josh Wade, and David Flaherty. They were divorced, young and very out-going, but just didn't seem to have that killer element either. If any of those six had committed the murders, they were very good at disguising any signs of the greed and hatred one would need to pull off such acts of violence.

They would delve into the backgrounds of

each of them to see if there were any underlying issues that were not apparent on the surface. Townsend's gut was telling him that that scenario was unlikely, but they could not rule it out.

Back at headquarters, Townsend had his team do background searches on the remaining six potential suspects. He also assigned someone to look into the backgrounds of the Irick's and Mr. Stephenson to see if their paths had ever crossed that could link them to an outsider that wanted them dead. It would take some time to collect all the data and review it, but they had no other leads in which to focus their investigation.

Collins looked at Townsend with that inquisitive look he often gets when he's got an idea. Townsend didn't have to ask; he knew that Collins would spit it out.

"I find it strange that the Hillard's had put a stipulation in their plan that whoever the recipient of their estate was, they were not allowed to sell the property. Why would they care since they would be gone anyway? And could there be someone wanting to buy the property for the sole purpose of building a commercial structure?" Collins might just have found another lead to pursue.

"You could be on to something Jack. I think we need to talk to the Hillard's again to see if anyone has approached them to purchase their property. The property does have a huge water frontage on the Intercoastal and with the four acres of land, there's plenty of room to build a restaurant or condos." Townsend grabbed his jacket and motioned for Jack Collins to follow him. They needed talk to the Hillard's right away.

CHAPTER TWELVE

D enise McNeely had been watching the news relating to the recent deaths of three people in the Banana Bay Beach Resort Community. That was next to where she had approached the Hillard's to offer to purchase their estate. She didn't know any of the deceased but knew in the back of her mind that their demise could work to her benefit.

She had contracted Angie Snowden to find a way to persuade the Hillard's to sell their property. She also knew that Angie had no qualms about how she got the job done. Denise pondered the idea that Angie could be behind these murders but didn't think she'd go quite that far. It would be a huge coincidence if Angie had nothing to do with what was going on over at Banana Bay Beach community.

Denise could be cold hearted at times when a deal was in the works. She'd step over anyone to close a deal. She didn't care what happened to those folks in Banana Bay as long as it could be advantageous to her. And right now, the three recent deaths could prove to work quite nicely in her favor.

Thankfully, she had told Angie to spare her any details on how she planned to persuade the Hillard's into buying. At least it couldn't be connected to her in any way. She wasn't sure whether to contact Angie or not to find out what her involvement, if any, was in the deaths of those three people. After a few minutes of thought, she figured the less she knew the better.

Maybe it was time to approach the Hillard's again to see if they had changed their minds about selling. She thought now was a little too soon but would definitely plan another visit to the Hillard's in about a week or so.

CHAPTER THIRTEEN

There was a knock on the Hillard's door so Will looked out the window to see that Agents Townsend and Collins had returned. They had already told them everything they could think of and didn't understand why they would be back so soon.

Opening the door, Will immediately stated his question. "I'm surprised to see you back so soon. Do you have any new information on what happened to Lyle?" Seeing their pause in response to his question, Will asked them to come in and have a seat.

Once seated at the kitchen table, Sally asked if they would like anything to eat or drink which they declined. Townsend looked at her and smiled then looked back to Will.

"It has come to our attention that you plan to hold a lottery in which one of a group of friends of yours will inherit your estate once you're gone."

"Yes, that's correct." Will responded with a puzzled look on his face.

"Has anyone approached you prior to the death of the Irick's and Lyle Stephenson asking you to sell your property?" Collins question was direct. Will and Sally looked at each other and then back at the Agents.

"As a matter of fact, a couple weeks prior to Thomas and Ginger's deaths, a real estate broker had stopped by and said she wanted to buy the property and that she would pay top dollar for it. I was angry that she just showed up without calling or anything and told her that we weren't interested in selling and that we were definitely not willing to sell to some developer."

"So, you do have a stipulation in your plan that whoever receives your estate is not allowed to sell it, is that correct?" Townsend asked.

"Yes, we did stipulate that. We want the place to stay the way it is and therefore, no one could sell out to a developer. Everyone agreed that the place should remain the way it is."

"Did the real estate broker know anything about your arrangement with your friends?" Collins asked.

Will was adamant. "No, I didn't say anything to her, nor would I and I don't know where she could ever get the information. Do you think she could be behind the murders?" Will asked. Sally practically collapsed onto the floor. "Oh my God, are we the reason our friends were murdered?" She was sobbing as Will tried to console her.

"No, no" Townsend said. "Do not blame yourself for anything that has happened. All we're trying to do is determine why someone would want these three friends of yours dead. We're following every lead that we can think of. But please, do not blame yourselves. Whoever killed your friends is to blame. We aren't even sure if the two cases are related yet."

"We understand Agents. It's just been so difficult these last few weeks." Will said putting his arm around his wife's shoulder.

"Just one more question. Can you give me the name of the real estate person that had come by?" Townsend took out his notepad.

"Yes, her name was Denise McNeely. She owns McNeely Real Estate Development. She gave me her card, but I threw it away. I think her office is in Orange Beach."

"Thanks so much for your help. We'll keep you posted of any new developments and if you think of anything else that might be useful, please don't hesitate to call." Jack handed Will his card. Will showed them to the door then returned to his wife who was still visibly upset.

"Oh Will, do you think our friends were killed because of this lottery we're planning? I just couldn't bear it if I thought we had brought all of this on." She was sobbing once again.

"Now Sally, you heard the Agents, they're not even sure if the two cases are linked. We just need to let them do their job and, in the end, we'll find out that we had nothing to do with what happened." That is what he told his wife, but he couldn't help but think that all three murders had occurred not long after they had told everyone of their plan to have the lottery. He prayed that he was wrong since he knew his loving wife would never forgive herself it that were true.

Townsend and Collins had left the Hillard's house with a renewed confidence that the three murders were, indeed, connected. They looked up McNeely Real Estate Development and drove the few miles along the coast to a large building that housed the business. It was obvious from the look of the place that Denise McNeely was doing very well in the real estate business.

They pulled into a slot near the front entrance, exited the car and walked inside to an elegantly furnished reception area. A woman was sitting behind a desk and asked if she could help them. After identifying themselves, they asked if Denise McNeely was available.

The receptionist looked puzzled and then got up and went inside a large office just off to the right. A few moments later, Denise came out of the office and greeted the two agents.

"Hello, I'm Denise McNeely, I understand you want to speak with me." Townsend flashed his badge and introduced himself and Agent Collins.

"Yes, if it's no trouble, we'd like to ask you a few questions regarding a case we're working on" Townsend said. There was a definite change in Denise's demeanor, but she cordially invited them into her office and shut the door.

"Please have a seat" she said waving her hand toward two overstuffed chairs that faced her huge mahogany desk. Both men sat down and continued to watch for any signs that Denise was uncomfortable with their presence. She maintained a stoic expression then asked how she could help.

"We're investigating the murders of Mr. and Mrs. Irick as well as Lyle Stephenson" Townsend said.

"Oh my" Denise replied. "Such a terrible thing that happened to those people. But I don't know what I could possibly tell you to help." Collins leaned slightly forward.

"We understand that you approached Mr. and Mrs. Hillard with an offer to buy their estate. Is that correct?"

"Well yes I did. But I was told by Mr. Hillard that they were not interested in selling. I was ready to offer top dollar. I was hopeful that I would be able to develop a luxury condominium complex on their property, but Mr. Hillard made it perfectly clear that he would never sell to a developer. So, I left. What could that possibly have to do with what happened to those people?"

"We have reason to believe that the murders of the Irick's and Mr. Stephenson could be related to the Hillard's property." Townsend stood and retrieved a card from his jacket pocket and handed it to Denise McNeely. "If you think of anything that may be helpful, please don't hesitate to call. Thanks for your time." Both men turned and left the office then got back in the car.

"So, what do you think?" Collins asked his partner. Townsend pondered the question for a bit.

"I'm not sure. If she is involved in the murders, she is very good at not showing it. She's a pretty cool cucumber and I find it hard to believe that she would just let go of a very lucrative investment after just one attempt."

"Yeah, we'll need to dig a little deeper into Mrs. McNeely. See if anything jumps out. Let's head back to headquarters and see if anyone has any leads. It was only a five-minute drive back to headquarters and Townsend was hoping that something had surfaced because they had nothing so far on who had committed three murders.

CHAPTER FOURTEEN

Friends arrived at the funeral for Lyle Stephenson, their expressions were of deep despair at the loss of another friend. As they approached the casket, their eyes gazed on a picture of Lyle as they had known him. Lyle was a handsome man with medium length light hair that suited his beach-life style. He had always been an avid outdoorsman. He loved boating, cycling and anything that would take him outdoors.

It was so surreal standing next to the closed casket of another close friend who died under strange circumstances. They could not allow their thoughts to dwell on the fact that three of their good friends were gone. That someone had taken their lives for no good reason. Their lives had been changed in the blink of an eye in a manner that no one should have to endure.

Detectives Townsend and Collins had attended the funeral, as well, and were seated near the back. Detective Collins had known all the victims in passing and was mourning their loss as was each of the friends. But their main objective to being there was to observe the crowd to see if anyone seemed suspicious or out of place.

They were curious to see if Denise McNeely would show up, but she hadn't. When the service was over, the detectives were no closer to identifying a viable suspect. But Denise McNeely was not off their radar yet. They would need to look into her past to see if she was involved in any kind of scandalous activity. It was their only lead, at this point.

Detectives Townsend and Collins planned to attend the interment in the event that they would discover a potential suspect there. As they watched the people exit the funeral home, it was obvious that Lyle Stephenson had touched many hearts in his community. But those that seemed touched the deepest, other than his mother who was deeply distraught, were his group of friends that had gathered near one of their cars.

Mrs. Hillard was sobbing into her husband's shoulder while the others tried to comfort her. A couple of them were whispering to each other but could not be over-heard by the detectives. It was plain to see that they were having difficulty understanding who could have wanted their friend's dead and if they, themselves, could be in danger. Something needed to surface fast before anyone else was killed. They had to find the connection to a suspect. And right now, they only had one in mind.

CHAPTER FIFTEEN

Upon arrival back at headquarters, Detective Townsend was anxious to see if any new leads had been discovered. Much to his disappointment, his team had yet to find any credible lead that would identify a suspect. The case was baffling. But there was one lead that had yet to be investigated. Townsend assembled his team in the conference room.

"Detective Collins and I just came from the funeral of Lyle Stephenson in order to surveil the attendees for suspicious actions. We found nothing. However, we have reason to believe that Denise McNeely could be involved in that she had made an offer to the Hillard's to buy their estate and was vehemently denied. We need to look deep into her past to see if there is anything that is similar or could lead us to a connection." Townsend took a couple questions and then dismissed his team to find a killer.

After a few hours, the team had done an extensive background check on Denise McNeely, her business and her husband Bruce. Detective Meyer spoke first.

"It turns out that Denise McNeely got her initial start in the real estate business with the help of her husband Bruce McNeely. He owns a fleet of corporate jet charter planes and has done quite well. Denise's business was slow to get going but she finally began making big money. However, about two years ago, the market took a down-turn and she lost a huge chunk of cash in the aftermath. I was able to find out that she went back to her husband for financial assistance but was denied because of feasibility of pouring more money into her failing business."

"Well, that certainly would make her motivated to find another source of revenue. She mentioned that the Hillard property would allow her to build a luxury condominium complex which would insure plenty of investor money. It would put her back on track, for sure" Townsend said.

"That certainly could be seen as a motive to persuade the Hillard's to sell" Collins said.

"I agree" Townsend replied. "We need to keep tabs on her and delve further into her past. Even before she was married and started her business to see if there are any sketchy incidents in her past. Also, check to see if she's had any prior business partners."

Townsend dismissed the group once again

to continue their investigations into McNeely's past, including her husbands. It would take some time to do a thorough investigation, but Townsend and Collins seemed confident that their diligence would lead to some evidence to support their theory; which was only a theory so far.

CHAPTER SIXTEEN

The Hillard's had invited their friends to go back to their house after the funeral service of their friend Lyle. It was a somber get-together, but everyone was there.

"Let us toast to our dear friends, Lyle, Thomas and Ginger, who would not want us to grieve for them. They would want us to carry on as if they were still here. But they *will* truly be missed." Will raised his glass as did the rest of the group.

"Cheers" the group shouted to the skies.

The gathering continued throughout the afternoon and other mourners had stopped by to celebrate the life of the departed. The close-knit group could not help but speculate on why their friends had been targeted in such a brutal manner. Although it went unsaid, it was clear that the remaining band of nine thought that the reason for the death of their friends could have something to do with the Hillard lottery. They just didn't know what.

There was a great deal of food that had been

brought to the Hillard's to feed the huge number of mourners who stopped by to pay their condolences. By 7pm, everyone had left except for Josh Wade, Dave Flaherty, Frank and Phyllis Barber and Angie and Sean Callen. They joined the Hillard's outside on the patio where very little conversation was taking place. Finally, Frank Barber broke the awkward silence.

"Is it just me, or does anyone else feel like there might be a connection to our friends' deaths and this lottery?" At the sound of Frank verbalizing what she had also thought, Sally broke down in tears.

"I knew this had something to do with this damn lottery. We've gone and gotten three of our dear friends killed over it." Immediately everyone tried to reassure Sally that there was nothing she could have done to prevent what had happened. They were all just speculating and knew that when the police found out who was responsible, she would know that it had nothing to do with her, Will and the lottery.

Everyone looked at Frank with a *why did you have to go and say that* look. They knew he didn't mean anything accusatory about it. Hell, they had all wondered the same thing. They just hadn't voiced it out loud.

The group finally decided to go when Will said he was going to get Sally something to help her sleep. He thanked them all for coming and reassured Frank that what he said was something they had already contemplated. They all agreed to keep in close contact with each other and to watch each-other's backs. It was a scary thought, but one they all took seriously.

Once everyone was gone, Will helped Sally to bed and gave her a sleeping pill that he knew would not relieve the anxiety she was feeling or give her a restful night's sleep. He knew it would be the same for him too.

CHAPTER SEVENTEEN

Friday night was usually an evening of festivities for David Flaherty. He had been invited to join some friends at their favorite hangout called Cobalt. It was an upscale restaurant that catered to the locals and the tourists during the summer. But he just wasn't in the mood to go out.

He received a welcomed call from a casual friend of his who had also wanted him to meet her out somewhere for a cocktail. Angie had met David through a mutual friend. He explained to her, Angie Snowden, that he was down in the dumps and just didn't feel like going out. Instead, she asked him if he'd like her to come over and hang out at his place. He didn't know her very well but had taken a liking to her when they were introduced. He did want to get to know her better but hadn't had the opportunity to pursue a relationship with her.

She expressed her concern over him being alone when he was so down in the dumps. He agreed that it might be a good idea not to be alone. She said she'd be over around six o'clock and would cook him some dinner. That actually sounded pretty good to him and told her he looked forward to seeing her soon. It was a chance to get to know her better and he could use that distraction in his life right now.

At just before six, Angie knocked on the brightly painted door of David Flaherty's house. She had been there once before with their mutual friend and had hoped that a relationship with David would blossom into something more.

He opened the door and welcomed her in. He managed a slight smile for her but deep down, he wasn't feeling very happy. She hoped to change that in the course of the evening.

"Come on in Angie. It's really nice of you to come over and keep me company. I'm afraid it won't be much fun for you though."

"Don't be silly David. What you need is for me to cook you some dinner and lend an ear if you need to talk about anything. I'm just here for you David. You're a good friend and I want to help you get through your pain." David wondered why she would think they had become good friends since he had only met her a few times, but she sounded very sincere and David felt that having her there was probably the best thing for him at the moment.

Angie brought along the fixings for a spaghetti dinner with rolls and salad. She busied herself in the kitchen while David opened a bottle of wine that she had also brought along. He poured them both a glass and sat at the kitchen counter while she prepared the meal. He felt very comfortable with her; something that had been lacking in his life since his wife passed.

They made small talk and drank more wine and before he knew it, he was starting to feel better. He was grateful for her insistence on coming over. As it turned out, she was able to bring him out of his doldrums to the point where he was actually talking and laughing with her. He welcomed the change of demeanor.

She served dinner in the dining room and they ate and drank till they were full. After clearing the dishes and loading the dishwasher, they retreated to the living room and shared more wine. David typically wasn't a wine drinker but the more he drank this evening, the more he liked it.

They sat intimately on the sofa and talked about anything that came to mind. Angie had turned on the stereo and they listened to some soft jazz. David was relaxed and in a good place when Angie leaned in and kissed him on the mouth.

At first, David was startled since they had never had a romantic relationship before. But that only lasted a moment until he kissed her back. Their passion was heating up and they both knew where it was headed. Just then, David stopped and sat upright.

"What's wrong David?" Angie asked as she righted herself on the sofa.

"I don't know. It just seems wrong that I'm doing this when my friend just died" he replied.

Angie tried to quell his concerns and asked if he wanted to talk about it. David then spilled his guts about how he thought the lottery on the Hillard's house could be linked to the murders of three of his friends. Angie's curiosity was peaked.

"If that is the case David, you could be in danger."

"I'm not worried about me. I can take care of myself. I'm just wondering if Will and Sally should call off this lottery and just leave the place to charity or something."

"Do you think that they would consider that?" she asked. "Maybe they should just sell it so no one else gets hurt, if they think that might be the reason behind the murders?"

"I know they won't sell it. It's just speculation on all of our parts. It could just be random. They certainly wouldn't sell it unless they knew for sure that that was what was behind the killings." He wished he had never brought the subject up. He thanked Angie for coming over and told her that he was sorry he had ruined the evening. She stood up to go and kissed him on the lips.

"You didn't ruin anything David. I had a

lovely evening. I hope we can do it again real soon. I do really like you." With a quick peck on the cheek, she walked to the door as he held it open for her, smiled and left.

David closed the door and went back into the living room to finish his drink. He could've kicked himself for acting like such a cry baby. He was pleased that she liked him and wanted to get together again as something more than just friends. He liked her too and was grateful that she was there for him tonight.

CHAPTER EIGHTEEN

Denise pondered the idea of going to the Hillard's to pitch her offer once more. She needed to see if the recent circumstances had swayed their opinion on selling their property. Best to strike while the iron is hot. She gathered her briefcase with her written proposal inside. If they wouldn't talk to her, she could leave the proposal with them. Maybe they might reconsider.

She arrived at the Hillard's at 3pm on Tuesday. She knocked on the door and waited a couple minutes before the door opened. It was Sally Hillard who answered.

"Hello, Mrs. Hillard? I'm Denise McNeely. I stopped by several weeks ago and talked to your husband about selling your property to me. Did he happen to mention it to you?" Sally looked at Denise with disdain.

"Yes, he did. He also said that he told you adamantly that we were not interested in selling."

"I understand. I know it was rather abrupt for me to just show up out of the blue. I just thought that after having time to think about it, the two of you might have had a change of heart. I brought along a written proposal of what I want to offer you for your property and would like for you to look it over. It's a very generous offer." Denise produced the proposal from her brief case and held it out to Mrs. Hillard.

"I'm sorry, but this is not a good time for us and I'm sure my husband was sincere when he told you that we weren't interested in selling."

"I understand that as well. However, with the recent murders that have happened in the neighborhood, I'm afraid that property values could take a hit and greatly devalue your property. I'm still ready to offer top dollar even with what has happened recently." Denise handed the proposal to Sally who reluctantly took it. Denise could see the pain on the old woman's face and thought that there might still be a chance to close the deal. But she needed to tread lightly.

"Just look over the proposal and if you're interested, please give me a call. By the way, did you happen to know the victims of the recent brutality personally?" She knew that hit a cord with Mrs. Hillard by the expression on her face. She didn't push it.

"Please, this is not a good time. I'll give this to my husband and if he has any interest, which I seriously doubt, we'll let you know."

"That's all I ask. Thanks for your time Mrs.

Hillard." Denise turned and left when Mrs. Hillard closed the door.

Will Hillard had been outside on the patio when Sally entered the kitchen and laid the proposal on the kitchen table. She walked outside and told Will that Denise McNeely had just dropped off a proposal to purchase the property.

"What the hell is with that woman anyway?" he said with a scowl. The nerve of her to show up here again after I told her that we would never sell to a real estate developer. The sadness he saw in his wife's face made him go to her and hug her.

"Maybe this place is cursed. Maybe we should just sell it" she said.

"You can't be serious" Will rebutted. Sally looked at her husband, tears welling in her eyes.

"I don't know Will. If this whole lottery thing is what got our friends killed, I couldn't bear to face them. Maybe we should just sell and go somewhere else so no one else gets hurt." She really didn't believe what she was saying, but the grief she was feeling was so overwhelming, she didn't know what to do.

"No Sally. This has nothing to do with wanting one of our friends to inherit this place. I refuse to sell what we have worked so hard to achieve all these years on the slight chance that there is a connection to our friend's deaths."

Sally knew when she was defeated and dropped the subject.

"Ok Will, whatever you say. I'm going to go in and make some dinner." She kissed her husband on the cheek then went inside.

Will was beside himself with anger that his wife was so distraught that she could possibly consider selling and moving away. He would have none of it. He would never sell, especially to Denise McNeely. If they had to cancel the lottery, they would. But he would not succumb to the vile creature, Denise McNeely, that would prey on his wife at such a vulnerable time.

Denise returned to her office with a renewed sense of hope. The key to persuading the Hillard's to sell would be with Mrs. Hillard. She was the weak link. Maybe she could talk her husband into selling. She was not ready to give up yet.

CHAPTER NINETEEN

Townsend got a call from one of their surveillance guys who had been tasked with keeping tabs on Denise McNeely. He informed him that Denise had gone over to the Hillard's around three. He said that he saw her leave some paperwork with Mrs. Hillard but didn't know what it was. He assumed it was some kind of offer to purchase their property.

He said that she was only there for about five minutes but said that Mrs. Hillard did take the paperwork. Townsend had a gut feeling that Denise McNeely was, somehow, involved in the three murders. He just had no way to prove it.

Maybe she was just trying to capitalize on a bad situation, but he didn't think so. They were getting nowhere fast and he had to change that.

The background check on Denise and her husband had provided no evidence of any shady business dealings in the past. That didn't mean that she wouldn't go to extremes to achieve what she wanted. She was definitely a determined woman. But would she go as far as to commit three murders to get there? That was a question that he could not answer.

Denise did, however, have communications with some people with questionable backgrounds. She was a partner with another real estate developer for a while that didn't pan out. They would question him.

She also had dealings with a woman who did some research and development for her company in the past. Her name was Angie Snowden. Everything they found on her left them questioning her morals, but there were never any criminal charges against her either. They would need to check into her a little deeper as well.

They also had a witness that said she saw a pickup truck in the general vicinity when Lyle was killed but couldn't give a good description which was pretty much useless at that point. There were three murders involving victims that lived in the same community which couldn't be a coincidence.

The question arose if a serial killer could be behind the murders. If that were the case, it would have to be someone that lived in the area. But serial killers usually kill in the same manner whereas these three killings were entirely different. It just didn't fit the MO of a serial killer. But nothing could be ruled out.

If the killings actually had nothing to do with the Hillard lottery, then they were barking up the wrong tree. There were so many questions and they were getting no answers. Someone had to know something. They just didn't know who.

Townsend and Collins sifted through everything they had, which was very little. There was no forensics from the boat explosion that killed the Irick's other than they knew a bomb had been planted on the boat. They needed to look deeper into that.

There was nothing that could lead to the hit and run driver other than a vague description of a truck that was in the general vicinity of Lyle Stephenson's death. They had to dig deeper and look for other witnesses. Whoever was behind these homicides was a professional if they were actually linked. They didn't even know that for sure. There were too many questions with no answers. But Townsend was not one to take no for an answer. He would find the information that would lead to whoever was behind these killings. Deep in his gut, he still thought Denise McNeely was at the center of it all.

It had been a week since the funeral of Lyle Stephenson. They had tried to track down the truck that had run him down with no success. If these killings were linked, whoever was carrying out the murders was very good. It was hard not to believe that the murders were linked to the Hillard estate. But there was nothing to lead to a suspect. They feared that the perpetrator was not finished.

The fact that the Hillard's were still not willing to sell could prove to be devastating. It was frustrating for the FBI team in that they still couldn't find a concrete clue to who was carrying out the deeds they believed Denise McNeely was behind. They weren't sure what steps to take to ensure no one else would be harmed because they had no clue who was carrying out the hits.

Someone knew more than they did and was using that to the advantage of the person who had most to gain from the murder of three of the Hillard's close friends. They had to find something that would lead them to the person that Denise McNeely hired to ensure her success in purchasing the Hillard property. They just had no leads to pursue.

CHAPTER TWENTY

Joshua Wade was a good friend and roommate of Lyle Stephenson. He had been very upset over losing his friend. Not only his roommate, but also his friends, the Irick's. He had been in a slump for several days and needed to move on. He had no idea how to do that.

Lyle had a twenty-six-foot Edgewater fishing boat that they had taken out on so many occasions over the past few years. It was housed at the Sportsman Marina. Josh thought that maybe taking the boat out for a day of fishing might improve his mood. He had many great memories of the times the two of them had taking it out on the gulf to fish and just have fun. Maybe what he needed was to go out and remember some of the good times.

He had been moping around the house for over a week and couldn't shake his grief. A day at sea might be just what he needed to break out of his slump. He had met Lyle through mutual friends which led them to sharing the property that Lyle had owned in the Banana Beach

Resort. They were both divorced and hit it off immediately.

They had similar experiences and enjoyed the same things. They had become very close over the time they spent together. They were just like brothers that neither of them had. Josh wanted to remember the good times they shared.

He called the marina and had them ready the boat for an afternoon launch. Lyle had put Josh's name on the list of people that could use the boat whenever they wanted so there was no issue with them prepping the boat for Josh when he called.

Josh packed a cooler with a few beers and sandwiches. The marina made sure there was bait on board along with all the fishing gear he would need. For the first time in days, Josh was upbeat about getting out and enjoying a day on the water like he and Lyle used to do.

He arrived at the marina at noon and the boat was waiting in a slip when he arrived. He talked to the staff at the marina and said he'd be out for a few hours but would have the boat back by 5pm. He loaded his cooler onto the boat and headed out across the bay toward the pass that would take him out on the open water of the gulf.

He and Lyle had a particular spot that they liked to fish which was about two miles off the coast. Once out on the open water, Josh pushed the throttle and set out at a steady pace. The water was calm, and the breeze was warm. It was just how he remembered it on many occasions in the past.

His spirits were already beginning to lift as he steered the vessel away from shore. The high-rise condos that lined the shore became smaller and smaller as he headed out away from shore. A few dolphins that were in the area seemed to ride along his wake. He opened a beer and continued another thirty minutes away from everything that had brought such sadness into his life recently.

The scent of the saltwater and the wind in his face made him feel as though everything was going to be just fine. Once he reached his mark, he throttled down to an idle. He cut the motor and dropped anchor. The condos along the shoreline were faint reminders of where he had been.

He set his fishing line and cast it out, securing it to its holder on the stern of the boat and sat back to wait for his first bite. The beer was cold and his memories of Lyle and himself doing exactly the same thing was a pleasant distraction. It really didn't matter if he caught anything today, he just wanted to remember the way it was. He was kicked back, enjoying the sun when he got his first bite. It was always exciting to catch a fish out on the ocean. He grabbed his reel and began working the fish in toward the boat.

Just before reeling the fish in, the line snapped. *No big deal* he thought. There'll be another one and popped open another beer. He fixed his line and cast it out again. It was a beautiful day. He had seen no other boats out where he was and figured all the fish would be for his taking.

He remembered back to when he used to fish with his father. He had grown up on the water and had loved every aspect of it. When his father had passed away, he hadn't had the opportunity to enjoy the water in the way that he had with his dad.

But when he met Lyle, he was able to resume his love for the water. Lyle had taken him out fishing many times and the two men had become close friends. Josh moved in with Lyle which had helped both of them financially. They had forged a friendship that had no bounds. Lyle was like a brother that he had never had. He cherished the fun times they shared and now that Lyle was gone, he was lost.

A faint hum of a motor made him look toward shore. He could see a boat in the distance but that didn't concern him. He was surprised that there were so few boats out that day. But the ocean was big enough for all of them. As the boat got closer, he could see it was a similar vessel as the one he was on and wondered if he knew who it was. He paid no mind to him and just enjoyed himself.

Back at the marina, the staff was preparing to receive the twenty-six-foot Edgewater that was due back in fifteen minutes. Josh would only need to drop off the boat where he had picked it up and the staff would take care of the rest.

The manager of the marina knew Josh and Lyle very well and knew that they always had the boat back when they said they would. But at 5pm, Josh had not returned the boat. They assumed he had lost track of time and would be along shortly.

At 6pm, Josh still had not returned and had not called to say he would be late. It wasn't much of a concern, but it was unlike either of them to not call ahead. After another hour passed and Josh still had not returned, they radioed his boat but got no answer. That was very unusual. After another hour passed with no communication, the marina owner notified the coast guard that they potentially had a missing vessel.

Josh had told the marina staff where he was headed and when no communication could be made, the coast guard decided to search for the vessel while it was still daylight. If it wasn't for the consistent adherence to the time frames involved in taking and returning the boat at the times agreed to, that Josh and Lyle had always abided by, there wouldn't be any question. But never had either of them taken out a boat without notifying the marina if they would be returning late. Nor have they ever not responded to the ship to shore radio communications.

The wind was picking up which kicked up the waves. There was a potential storm later that evening which would end their search if they didn't find Josh before then. They also knew that any experienced boater would heed the warnings of an oncoming storm. There was definitely something that wasn't right.

After an hour of searching the area where Josh said he was going, they spotted the vessel seemingly bobbing on the water and pulled alongside.

They could not see anyone on board. The vessel was still anchored in place but there was no sign of Josh. Once on board, they could see his fishing line still in the water, but Josh was nowhere to be found. They reeled the line in and then contacted the marina to tell them that they had found the boat, but no one was on board. They searched the area for a half mile radius but still saw no sign of Josh.

They towed the boat back to the marina and contacted the police to report that Joshua Wade was missing. There was no way that Josh would have left the boat out in the water like that. They got a forensics team to check the boat for anything that could determine if there was any foul play involved. Nothing seemed to be out of place other than the fact that Joshua Wade was not on board. Finally, they found a small speck of blood near the bow but nothing else.

Josh's cell phone was found in the glove compartment on the boat and it showed no attempts to call anyone. It was now dark and an official missing person's report was filed for Joshua Wade.

News spread quickly of his disappearance and dread filled the hearts of those that knew him. Speculation was that he had possibly fell overboard and drowned but that did not ease the anguish of those that knew and loved him.

Two days passed as the coast guard searched for him in the waters where the boat was found to no avail. Late in the afternoon of the third day, a fisherman fishing from the beach had made a gruesome discovery. His hook had caught onto something that he thought was a big catch when in fact, when he reeled it in, it was a human arm.

Immediately, the police were called and arrived on scene. The fisherman was identified as Dewey Long, a long-time resident of the area and avid gulf fisherman. Dewey had said that he often fished from the beach along the Orange Beach coast.

He was sitting on the beach with his head between his hands. The sight of the arm was utterly shocking, but what he noticed on the hand caused an overwhelming sadness throughout his body.

When questioned by law enforcement, he

said that he might know who the arm belonged to. There was a tattoo of a shark on the hand of the arm he had reeled in. He was pretty sure he recognized the tattoo. A friend of his had an identical tattoo on his left hand. Tears welled in Dewey's eyes as he had a horrible feeling that the arm he reeled in belonged to Josh Wade.

It turned out to be the left arm and hand of a human. The forensics team were brought in and the body part was taken to the Medical Examiner's office where it was determined that the arm had, in fact, belonged to Joshua Wade.

The news media went rampant with the news and upon further examination by the ME, it was apparent that there were signs that the wrist had been bound. The ME ruled the incident as a homicide. No other body parts were ever found but they had determined that there were signs that the arm could have been separated from the body by a shark or boat propeller.

The whole community was alarmed that a shark could have killed Joshua Wade, but the ME's report said that the body had most likely been bound and put into the water and drowned. The shard attack had occurred post-mortem. Someone had bound Josh's wrists and possibly his legs and dumped him overboard to drown.

This was now the fourth murder of a resident of the Banana Bay Beach Community. This was not a coincidence.

CHAPTER TWENTY-ONE

Townsend and Collins were immediately notified of the fourth homicide of a resident
of the Banana Bay Beach Resort. They arrived
at the marina the following morning and began interviewing the staff. They were told that
Josh had called the day before to have Lyle's
boat ready for launch around noon. It was not
unusual for Josh to take out the boat since Lyle
had given Josh the permission to use his boat on
fishing excursions.

Everything seemed normal was what they
had told the Agents. They told them that Josh
had taken out the boat several times before and
had always returned when he said he would.
They said that when Josh had not returned on
time, they didn't think much of it. But when
hours passed and he hadn't returned, nor could
they reach him by radio, they knew something
wasn't right. That was when they called in the
coast guard to check it out.

Townsend had a strange feeling that this
was the second time a boat was taken out from

the Sportsman Marina that ended in tragedy. It would need to be investigated further. The Irick's had also housed their boat at the Sportsman Marina and it had resulted in blowing up. Now, Josh takes out another boat, and he is dead. Maybe there is something strange going on with this marina. However, it doesn't connect with the hit-and-run death of Lyle Stephenson. This case was becoming more and more bizarre.

Will and Sally Hillard had been sitting out by the fire when they came inside to watch a little TV before going to bed. They always watched the 10 o'clock news before retiring when the breaking news announced that a body part had been brought ashore by a gulf fisherman. The name was not being released until family was notified. They had no idea that the arm belonged to their dear friend Josh Wade. It wouldn't be until hours later that they learned what had happened.

They didn't find out until the next day that the arm had belonged to Josh. His mother and father had been notified and were flying down from Atlanta. Fear surged through the small community of the Banana Bay Beach Resort as now there were four people dead from their community.

Panic was beginning to spread, and residents were afraid to leave their homes. Speculation was soaring through the community that a serial killer was preying on the residents. Calls were coming into the police station asking what was being done to protect them and to find the killer. There were no answers. Some residents left to visit relatives in other area in fear for their lives. No one could give them answers.

The news hit the Hillard's hard as they realized another of their lottery friends had just been killed. They were at wits end on what to do. They had to mourn the death of another of their dear friends, and they feared that they were to blame.

Sally was beside herself with guilt. No matter how much Will tried to console her, she would not believe that they had not been the cause of all of it. They argued over what to do and Sally said that the lottery was off. She could not bear to think that four of their friends had died because of them. The only thing left to do was cancel the lottery.

They called the remaining members of the lottery and told them that they felt that this lottery had led to the death of their friends but didn't understand why. Everyone agreed.

The service was held three days later. Will and Sally Hillard had arrived but when they greeted their friends, they felt there was some animosity towards them. Sally understood why they would feel that way even though they had all been friends for such a long time. They knew that their friends now blamed them for the deaths of four of their neighbors and friends. She could hardly bare to face them.

Will tried to console her but he also knew now that this was not the work of some serial killer that was randomly killing people in their close-knit community. He knew that they had set this course of devastation in motion and had no way to not except responsibility. They felt that anyone that was close to them was a potential victim and their friends felt the same way.

Life at the Hillard house would no longer be the same. The fun atmosphere that they had provided for so many years and turned into a death trap. The parties that they held almost every weekend stopped. Sally fell into a deep depression. Will had no idea how to fix it. Life was falling apart. They were to the point that maybe it would be better if they just moved away. Maybe no one else would die.

When someone leaked to the media that there was a lottery for the Hillard estate and those that had been part of it were dropping like flies, it was the last straw for Sally and Will. The residents of the Banana Bay Beach Resort, those that were not part of the lottery, began to feel a bit at ease thinking that they were not the target of some deranged killer. The weight of it all only added to the depression that Sally had already fell into.

The only thing that Will could do was to notify the media that the lottery was cancelled. It was an effort to stop the killings that so many people had associated the lottery with. The once strong bond that the band of nine had with the Hilliard's was broken. The life that they all shared over the years was no more. Shame and disgrace fell upon the Hilliard's and they were left to live a life of despair. Neither of them could take it any longer.

CHAPTER TWENTY-TWO

D enise McNeely watched the news of the latest broadcast of the death of Joshua Wade and wondered in the back of her mind what was happening to move things in her direction. There was only one answer. She had hired Angie Snowden to do whatever it took to persuade the Hillard's to sell their property.

She had no idea that Angie would go this far, but she was almost sure that she was behind it. Fate did not step in and cause four people to die that could inherit the Hillard place so she could step in and buy it. No, Angie had gone way too far. But the way she saw it, it would be Angie's ass on the line, not hers.

She did not instruct Angie to kill those people. All she did was tell her to do whatever was necessary to get the Hillard's to sell. Would that make her an accomplice? She didn't think so. If Angie was exposed as being behind the murders, could it be linked back to her? She had to know if Angie had orchestrated the deaths of those four people. She would need to make the call.

Sitting at her desk, she didn't really want to know, but she had to protect herself. If Angie arranged to have those people killed, they might be able to link Angie back to her. She picked up the phone and dialed Angie's number. After three rings, Angie picked up.

"Hello Denise. How are you?"

"Quite frankly, I'm a little concerned. There have been four murders of the lottery people and I'm wondering if you had anything to do with it?"

"Relax" Angie replied. "Nothing can be traced back to you. You told me to do whatever it took to get them to sell. I'm pretty sure they're starting to lean in that direction."

"I didn't think you'd resort to murdering four people. That's a little extreme don't you think?"

"Well, I didn't see any other way. I have a friend who is one of the lottery contenders and he said that even after the first three, he didn't think they'd sell. But he said that they felt that the lottery was the reason for the killings and that they were thinking about calling it off. I just gave them a little push."

"The FBI agents that are on the case came to see me the other day. They know that I approached the Hillard's to offer to buy their place and they know that they turned me down. I'm afraid that they might think that I have something to do with the murders of those people."

"Don't worry. I'm sure you have an alibi for whenever the murders happened, and they'll never trace it back to you."

"Listen to me. I did not ask you to kill anyone."

"You hired me to do a job and you gave me full authority to do whatever it took. Don't worry. You'll be fine."

"I better be because I will not go down for this."

"Listen Denise don't threaten me. Just make sure you've got a big paycheck for me when that property is yours."

"Don't worry. When that property is mine, you'll be well compensated. I'll stand to make millions on the deal. I wish no one had to die, but so be it. Just make sure you don't screw up."

"Not a problem. Now just sit back and wait for opportunity to come to you." The phone went dead.

CHAPTER TWENTY-THREE

Townsend had his task force assembled in the conference room to see if there were any new developments.

"So, do we have anything good to report?" The group didn't look optimistic. But there was something. A detective sitting near the door spoke up.

"Forensics couldn't find anything on the boat to identify the perp and they did confirm that the blood spec was Joshua Wades. However, there was another boat in the area that saw two boats near each other. He didn't pay much attention to it because he was headed out further. He said he saw the Edgewater anchored about two hundred yards east of where he was and that there was another boat approaching it about fifty yards behind. He was pretty sure it was about a twenty-three-foot Cobia, center console. He was moving away from them so didn't pay much attention, but the Cobia was coming up on the Edgewater. That was all he could say."

"OK, let's check all the marinas for anywhere

between a twenty and twenty-three-foot Cobia that may have been rented for the day. If that was our killer, he probably didn't own the boat, but check owners of the same. Anything on Denise McNeely's activity?"

"We only have a warrant to check her phone activity. She did call Angie Snowden yesterday and had about a five-minute conversation" a detective said.

"We need to put surveillance on Angie Snowden. She could be the one doing the dirty work for Denise McNeely. What do we know about this Angie Snowden?" Townsend asked.

"She's got a rap sheet that says she's been involved in some distortion and other minor issues. Not anything that would say she's a gun for hire. But we've had people that have jumped from minor charges to bigger things before. I wouldn't rule her out as a person of interest."

"Let's bring her in and see what she has to say."

A police cruiser was sent to Angie Snowden's known address. They knocked on her door but there was no answer. They called out but still no one answered the door. They would sit on her house until she returned. At that time, they would politely ask her to come to the station to answer some questions. The key would be in her response. If she was combative and hesitant, that would be a sign she had something to hide.

About thirty minutes into the surveillance, Angie pulled into her driveway and began unloading groceries. They waited for her to finish, then, once again, knocked on her front door. A few moments later, Angie opened the door. The officers explained why they were there and asked if she would come to the station to answer some questions. Angie smiled and agreed to follow them to the station. No hesitation at all.

An hour later after the request, Angie Snowden was sitting across from Agents Townsend and Collins. She seemed calm and polite when Townsend told her why they asked her to come in.

"Ms. Snowden, do you know a Denise McNeely?" Townsend asked. They already knew she had a conversation with her in the past couple days. They wanted to see if she lied about it.

"Yes, I know Denise. I've done some research for her in the past." Collins was almost disappointed that she told the truth.

"What kind of research?" he asked.

"She's hired me in the past to research different properties to see if they would be a good investment for development. Stuff like that."

"Did she have you do any research on a property owned by Will and Sally Hillard?"

"No, she's never asked me to look into that property. I usually research properties that are already on the market. I don't believe the Hillard house is listed for sale."

The questioning continued for another thirty minutes. They thanked Angie for her time and let her go. Townsend walked her to the door and watched as she left the building with not a care in the world.

"So, Collins, what do you think? Could she be a cold-blooded killer?"

"I didn't see any signs of distress or nervousness. If she had anything to do with the murders, she is one cool cucumber." Collins just shrugged his shoulders.

"Yeah, that's the feeling I got too. If she's involved, she has no conscience. Let's keep a tail on her for a few more days." Collins picked up the phone and made the request for surveillance. The only thing they could hope for now is that something develops with the boat that was seen near the area where Lyle's boat was found.

CHAPTER TWENTY-FOUR

After Angie Snowden left the office of Denise McNeely earlier that morning, she was a little pissed off that Denise had practically reprimanded her for doing the work she was hired to do. Did Denise think that Angie was just going to go and sweet talk the Hillard's into selling their estate to her? Not hardly. Fear was a great motivator and the Hillard's were older and more vulnerable. She figured once they connected the victims to the lottery, the Hillard's would be more than happy to rid themselves of the place that caused so much grief and misery.

But the Hillard's were a couple of tough birds and hadn't shown any tendency towards selling the place. She needed to find out where their mindset was, and she knew exactly the person who could tell her.

Her relationship with David Flaherty was developing and he was one of the participants in the lottery. He would have a good feel for how the Hillard's were dealing with the recent tragedies.

As luck would have it, David called Angie in hopes of taking her out to dinner. She gladly accepted his offer. He would pick her up at her place at 7pm.

David had contemplated on whether to ask Angie out. He missed his wife terribly, but it had been two years since she died. He wanted to move on but the guilt he felt kept him from jumping back into the dating scene.

But Angie seemed different. He enjoyed being around her. She was attractive, funny and something he really wanted back in his life. Finally, he made the decision and called. He was delighted that she accepted.

Angie actually had a fondness for David and felt a slight pang of guilt at using him to get information. But information was what she needed and if using David to get it was what it required, so be it. Once this whole ordeal was over and Denise purchased the Hillard estate, she would love to continue to date David.

Angie had a failed relationship several years back and had almost sworn off relationships. And it worked for quite a while. She dated guys for very brief periods of time and then broke it off. She vowed not to get involved seriously with anyone ever again.

She tried not to reflect on the past, but she knew that the bad relationships always seemed to start out good. It was only after she fell for them that their true colors had shown through. And those colors tended to be very dark shades of grey. She wanted to make sure that David would not fall into that category.

But David was different. She had known him for several months and had never seen any type of anger issues or anything remotely close to that. He was mild mannered, soft spoken, very handsome and built like a brick wall.

Even after they started to see each other more intimately, she never witnessed anything that could be construed as mean or hateful. He brought a renewed sense of acceptance that good men really do exist.

She was dressed and ready to go when her doorbell rang. David was standing there when she opened the door holding a bouquet of flowers and a big smile.

"Oh David, the flowers are beautiful. Come on in while I put them in a vase" she said stepping aside to let him in.

David followed Angie to the kitchen and watched as she placed the flowers in a glass vase she filled with water. "They're not near as lovely as you Angie" he said as he kissed her on the forehead. Angie blushed as she was not used to getting compliments such as that. One more reason to believe he might be worth a long-term relationship.

They left for dinner a few minutes later. They

had reservations at McGuire's Steak House in Pensacola. It was a popular restaurant which was only a ten-minute drive from where Angie lived. She had gone there on several occasions previously and always enjoyed the food.

They had a drink at the bar while they waited for their table. She wasn't sure how to brooch the subject of the Hillard's, so thought she'd wait till they had a couple more drinks. That always seemed to loosen one's tongue.

They were seated in a booth near the window that looked out over the parking lot. The place was beginning to fill up and they had been lucky to get a reservation on such short notice. The waiter took their order and brought them another round of drinks. They made small talk until the food arrived and ate without much conversation. The waiter cleared their plates when they were finished eating and asked if they'd like dessert. David ordered for both of them.

"So, David, I've been seeing all this craziness on the news regarding that lottery the Hillard's had going on. They must be devastated." David shook his head.

"This is really hard for them Angie. Sally is convinced that the lottery is the reason that the murders had taken place. She is beside herself with grief and guilt" he said.

"That's just terrible" Angie replied. "I can't

imagine what they are going through. And what about you David? You're part of that lottery. Aren't you afraid that you could be next?"

"Yeah, it's pretty scary. But Will and Sally cancelled the lottery so if the lottery was the reason for the murders, there shouldn't be any more. At least that's what we're all hoping."

"Have they decided what they were going to do with their estate now that the lottery is called off?" David looked at Angie with a questioning expression on his face. She hoped she hadn't pried too much.

"I saw them at Josh's funeral, and they couldn't bear to join us. I think they think that we all hate them for what's happened. But they couldn't have known that people would die over their generous wish for one of their friends to inherit their estate. I heard that they might move away because it's too difficult to face the rest of their friends and people in the community."

"That is such a shame that they would have to do that." She could see the sadness in David's face and tried to offer comfort. She had the information that she came for so decided not to push the questioning anymore. She didn't want him to think she was anything more than a concerned friend.

They ate their desserts and then left McGuire's. They decided to go to Cobalt for a few more cocktails and some dancing under the stars. There would be live music at the outside bar and Angie wanted to take David's mind off their previous conversation. Which is exactly what she did.

CHAPTER TWENTY-FIVE

Will and Sally Hillard had become reclusive after Josh's funeral. They couldn't convince themselves to face their dear friends. The guilt they felt compelled them to steer clear of all their friends in an effort to protect them from a fate that seemed to follow them wherever they went. They had decided to distance themselves from their friends which was one of the hardest things they had ever had to do.

The parties at their home were no longer a part of their weekly festivities. They sat in their house and feared for the welfare of the rest of their friends. Several of their friends had called to talk to them but they wouldn't answer the phone. It was a terrible way to live and it seemed to be taking a terrible toll on Sally.

Some of the others had gotten together after they noticed how distant the Hillard's had become. They knew of the guilt Will and Sally had been feeling and wanted to try and comfort them. Everyone knew that the lottery was the likely reason behind the murders, but Will and

Sally could not have known something like that would happen. Who would ever think something like that?

The five remaining friends and members of the, now defunct, lottery decided that they were going to go to the Hillard's and support them. They needed to bring Will and Sally out of the depression they were drowning in. The lottery was over and no one else would have to die. They would convince the Hillard's that it was time to move on and get back to the life they had enjoyed for so long. The parties had to restart, and they all needed to put the recent tragedies behind them.

It was decided that the remaining five would bring the party to the Hillard's and make them join in the festivities. It would be difficult for everyone; however, they knew their departed friends would want them to carry on. It was a collection of all of them that would keep the memories of Thomas, Ginger, Lyle and Josh alive. It was the right thing to do.

On Saturday, they all met at Angie and Sean's house. Appetizers were prepared and alcohol and beer had been purchased. Everything was loaded into one of the vehicles then they all headed to Sally and Will's house.

David knocked on the door and when Will answered, they all yelled out 'SURPRISE'. Will looked at the group and didn't quite understand what was happening. Sally heard the shout and went to the front door to see what the commotion was.

Before either one of them could object, Phyllis told them it was time to move on and that everyone was ready to get back to normal and that they would not take no for an answer.

Will and Sally looked at each other and smiled. They stepped aside to let everyone in. Hugs abounded and everyone carried the food and drink outside and began making cocktails and laying out the appetizers.

From the expression on Sally's face, it looked as though a huge weight had been lifted from her. The sullen and sad expression that had been the norm, was now bright with her usual brilliant smile spread across her face almost from ear to ear. Will had noticed it and walked over to his wife and hugged her to him. A swell of relief swept over him knowing that things were beginning to look up for their small family of friends.

Music filled the air and as was always the case, they prepped Will's boat for their sunset cruise along the intercoastal waterway. It was a rebirth that had happened to all of them. Once again, there was laughter and conversation as if the fun had never stopped.

Once out on the water, the evening sky was beginning to show its brilliant colors beginning to light up the night sky. It was going to be a brilliant sunset. Will and Sally had never felt so blessed to be surrounded by such good people; people they considered family. Life really could go on and everyone was safe now that the lottery had been cancelled.

CHAPTER TWENTY-SIX

D avid Flaherty had been in contact with Angie Snowden and had told her what the plans were for getting the Hillard's back in the game and out of their funk. He also told her that they were going to make sure that Will and Sally continued with the lifestyle they were used to and not to allow guilt to drive a wedge between the family.

Angie told David that what they were doing was a nice gesture, but deep down, she knew that could mean trouble for Denise McNeely. Angie was sure that the Hillard's were on the verge of selling their estate and had no doubt that Denise would persuade them to sell to her.

But this newfound resurrection from depression by the Hillard's could easily put an end to that. She didn't believe that the plan that David had laid out to her that day would actually work. How could the Hillard's possibly move on from causing the deaths of four of their dear friends. No one could overcome that.

But she played along to David so as not to

sound insensitive. Time would tell if their plan would work and she sorely doubted that it would. She would wait and call David the following day to see how their mis-guided loyalty to the Hillard's had turned out. She figured she was worrying for nothing.

The Hillard's were older and not in the best health. Certainly, the trauma of the murders had taken a permanent hold on their sanity and Angie's plan would ultimately prevail. Therefore, there was no need to inform Denise of this new ripple in their efforts. Denise would not take the information graciously, so Angie knew she needed to know for sure how the Hillard's reacted to the efforts to make them whole again.

Angie sat at home sipping a glass of wine and wishing she knew how things were going at the Hillard's. She wanted to call David but knew she had to bide her time. It was driving her crazy to the point she was pacing the living room floor willing the phone to ring with good news. But the phone didn't ring and after the second bottle of wine, Angie was ready to flop into bed and let the effects of the wine lull her off to sleep.

The morning would bring her good news and a throbbing headache to boot. Once her head hit the pillow, she was out like a light. She rested peacefully for six hours before waking to a loud banging in her head. The wine had reared its ugly head. She went to the bathroom and popped two aspirin then proceeded to brew a pot of coffee.

It was 8am, so it was a little early to call David for details of the previous evening. Besides, she had never called him that early before and didn't want to stir any up any suspicion. She would drink her coffee and have some breakfast to pass the time. Hopefully, David would call her instead of she having to instigate the conversation.

Just before 10am, the phone rang. Her cell showed the caller was David.

"Hey David, how are you this morning?" she asked with her cheeriest voice.

"Just great. I didn't want to call you too early, but it was killing me to wait any longer. Last night, remember I told you we were going over to the Hillard's to try and bring them out of the guilt slump?" Angie wasn't liking the excited tone of his voice.

"Yeah, I remember" she replied.

"Well, as it turns out, the Hillard's were so receptive to the group showing up and wanting to get things back to normal that we all hung out and partied then went out for our usual sunset cruise. It was great. Just like nothing had ever happened. Will and Sally said that they were so glad we all came over and that all they wanted was to get back to normal. Is that the best news ever?"

"Wow, David, that is great news." Angie's headache was getting worse after the news she had not wanted to hear. This was the worse outcome she could have hoped for. She was back at square one and knew exactly what that meant. Her work wasn't done yet.

CHAPTER TWENTY-SEVEN

Townsend's team had been scouring every marina within a twenty-mile radius in search of the phantom Cobia boat that was last seen approaching Joshua Wade's boat on the day he went missing. Finally, after hours and hours of searching, they found a marina near Pensacola that had rented out a twenty-three-foot Cobia center console.

The manager of the marina had provided the paperwork to the agents after they told him what their interest was. The name on the rental slip stated the boat was rented to a John Franklin. The boat had been picked up around 6am and had been returned that same evening around 6pm.

The manager stated that he was not at the marina when the boat was picked up and couldn't describe the man but said that one of the dock hands, Jeff Pass, was working that early and may have seen the guy when he picked up the boat.

Fortunately, Jeff was available and was called

up to the marina office where he was introduced to the agents. Jeff said he was on the dock when the guy picked up the boat. His description was a six-foot, white male with dark brown, short hair. He was wearing a blue wind jacket and dark blue ball cap. He didn't see the guys face very good as he seemed to keep his face in profile.

The agents thanked the men for their time and asked that if they remembered anything else, to please give them a call and handed both men their cards. They were excited about getting the name of their potential suspect and alerted Townsend that they were on their way back to headquarters with the information.

The team was assembled when the agents arrived and once everyone was present, they went over the details of the suspect. When all was said and done, Townsend had an uneasy feeling. It couldn't be that easy. Immediately he enlisted Collins to do a background check on John Franklin. Just as quickly, they ran into a problem.

The marina manager had said that the boat was rented over the phone and had only gotten his name and address but no credit card. When John Franklin arrived to pick up the boat, he paid in cash to the clerk who was on duty. She couldn't even remember anything about the guy. She said he dropped off the cash and signed the rental sheet then he left for the dock. The keys had already been put in the boat so very little contact was made between John Franklin and any of the staff at the Southwind Marina in Pensacola.

After an in-depth search on the name John Franklin and the address he had given, it was a dead end. The address was an old warehouse off Main Street and the name John Franklin was likely an alias. With no real description of John Franklin other than height, weight and hair color, there was nowhere to go from there. A promising lead turned out to be nothing but another dead end.

Although it had been well over a week since Joshua Wade went missing, Townsend still sent over a forensics team to go over the Cobia for any prints or evidence that could lead to the bogus John Franklin. But the manager had said the boat had been cleaned and rented out a few times since then, it was more like chasing your tail than identifying a suspect. Hours later, that exact result was confirmed. They would still try and identify the prints they did pull from the boat to eliminate them. It was a long shot, but maybe there would be a print that they couldn't eliminate as a suspect. Cases had been solved with less.

CHAPTER TWENTY-EIGHT

After hanging up the phone with David, Angie paced the kitchen with her coffee cup in hand. Her wine headache had finally subsided, but she knew another headache was not far off. She hadn't talked to Denise McNeely in over a week. When they last spoke, Denise was confident that the Hillard's were getting closer to selling their property.

Now, it seems that the Hillard's had had a change of heart due to their flock of friends. Angie cursed out loud at her new dilemma. She would need to let Denise know about the latest events that would put her future venture on hold. But it couldn't be put off. She needed to call Denise and fill her in and figure out what the next steps would be.

Reluctantly, Angie dialed Denise's private office number hoping that Denise wasn't available. Denise picked up on the second ring. Her voice was pleasant, but Angie knew that was about to change.

"Denise McNeely" she spoke into the phone.

"Hello Denise, this is Angie. How are you?"

"I'm doing great. What's up?"

"I'm afraid I have some bad news Denise. I spoke with my source on the current status of the Hillard house. It seems that the remaining group of Hillard friends have reinvigorated the Hillard's to the point that they've all decided to move on with their lives as if nothing had ever happened. In other words, the Hillard's have decided to stay where they are and don't have any plans to sell the property." Angie waited for the explosion on the other end. Much to her surprise, Denise remained calm.

"This is definitely a set back to my plans. However, I know how resourceful you are, and I expect that you will resolve this dilemma quickly." Denise wouldn't say anything incriminating, but she knew she made it clear to Angie what needed to be done.

"Alright" Angie replied. "I'll see what I can do to get things back on track. I assume you'll not want to know any of the details as before?"

"Absolutely not" Denise responded adamantly. "I want no knowledge of anything you've done or plan to do. What I need is plausible deniability. And what you need is to be very discrete. We already have the Feds asking us questions. You cannot afford to give them anything that could lead back to us. Understand?" Angie knew Denise was looking out for her own ass. And she understood that. However, Angie was taking all the risk and expected to be compensated accordingly.

"I understand completely." Angie hung up before she could hear Denise slam down the receiver on her end. Denise was livid with this new turn of events. It was like having to start all over again. Denise was used to getting what she wanted and when she wanted it. This delay did not sit well with where Denise had hoped she'd be at this point. But until the Hillard's were convinced to sell, there was nothing she could do but wait.

Angie was glad the call to Denise was over, but now she had to come up with something else to put the Hillard's back in the frame of mind necessary to achieve the goal set out by Denise. Angie was sure her man could pull off another hit if that was required. He had covered his tracks well before and knew she could count on his discretion and ability to do whatever was necessary.

Planning would be crucial. Angie wasn't sure what the next steps would be and every aspect of it had to be precise. She knew that the Feds were keeping an eye on her. She had noticed the tail on her on a couple of occasions. She didn't know the extent of their surveillance though. It was possible that they were tracking her calls, but she had covered that inquiry by telling the Feds about the research she did for Denise. It would explain away any phone calls she made to Denise.

New burner phones needed to be purchased for John Franklin, her man, just to keep the anonymity of his identity and association with herself in place. As long as they were unable to identify John as a suspect, there would be no way to track him back to her. In the event that ever happened, she had already devised a plan to ensure his silence.

With a renewed confidence about the situation, she went to the kitchen to fix some lunch. While she ate, she spread out her folder on the Hillard house to see if she could devise another event to revert the Hillard's back to their original state of mind before the party that David had attended. She really liked David a lot but was slightly ticked off that he had initiated the party that crippled her plans to reap a huge paycheck from Denise McNeely.

As she ate a sandwich of tuna salad she had made the previous day, she thought back to a time when life was much simpler. She wondered how her life had come to what it was now. Only five years ago she was working in the Corporate world. The money was pretty good, but the stress involved in the day to day dealings of high-powered executives did not suit her.

She wanted to be her own boss to have the mobility and flexibility that her previous job did not provide. Starting her own business in real estate research and development was a slow start. It took a couple years to build a client base and earn a decent income. But it wasn't until she met Denise McNeely two years prior, that the money stream had begun to flow.

Dealing with Denise was pretty straight forward in the beginning, but it didn't take long to see that Denise could be conniving and ruthless when it came to getting what she wanted. Angie had realized that it was very easy for her to adapt to the ways of Denise McNeely so much so that she had reinvented herself to the person she was today.

Angie had a few other clients that paid handsomely for her skills and she took advantage of each one. Her reputation on the dark web was well known and when people needed her services, they were willing to pay huge sums in insure discretion and completion.

What made it so easy for Angie to adapt was her ability to remove emotion from work. She felt no remorse for the things she did and became very good at her job. She had banked a boat load of money that was secured in an offshore account to the point that after this job with Denise was finished and she collected her cash, she was out of the business and off to some island yet to be chosen to enjoy the good life.

But first things first. She had to get the deal done.

CHAPTER TWENTY-NINE

The forensics team had been working solely on identifying fingerprints from the Cobia boat that was seen approaching Joshua Wade on the day he went missing. They had pulled over thirty sets of prints that the team had been trying to trace in order to eliminate them or determine if they could be persons of interest. So far nothing had panned out that could point a finger at a suspect.

Townsend and Collins were feeling the frustration mounting as no real leads were forthcoming. Whoever was behind the previous murders was very good at hiding their tracks. They had a hard time believing that Angie Snowden could have pulled the murders off herself. It was their combined opinion that she had enlisted a hired assassin to do the actual dirty work.

But even Angie was good at hiding any link to the murders. Their assumption was that Denise had hired Angie to help persuade the Hillard's to sell. When it couldn't be done by verbal offers, Angie hired John Franklin to take things to a whole new level. Murder for hire was the path Angie chose either with or without Denise McNeely's blessing.

The only problem was they had no evidence to prove their theory and they were unable to find this John Franklin. He was invisible. They had nothing but a vague description of him, the name John Franklin was an alias and they had not been able to identify any fingerprints, so far, that could lead to his real identity. If they could determine that, then the walls would start crumbling around Angie Snowden and Denise McNeely. It was a big IF.

Townsend and Collins decided to go see the Hillard's again to find out how they were doing and to see if they had remembered anything that might be helpful to the case. Before heading to the Hillard's, the agent that had been monitoring the phone transactions of Denise McNeely and Angie Snowden stopped them.

"Hey Townsend, just wanted to let you know that Angie Snowden made a call today to Denise McNeely's office phone. The call lasted about five minutes. We have no way of knowing what was said, but just thought you'd want to know. If we could get a warrant to listen in on the conversations, we might be able to catch them saying something incriminating" the agent said.

"Yes, we would, but unfortunately, we don't have enough evidence to get that. But keep an eye on Angie Snowden's phone activity. We need to see if she gets in contact with John Franklin. Track down who she calls to see if anyone suspicious jumps out. We need to find out who he is." Townsend thanked the agent then left with Collins.

It was a beautiful, sunny day when Townsend pulled up the driveway of the Hillard place. Will had been out front and immediately saw them as they pulled in the driveway. He put down his gardening shears and approached the agents as they exited the car.

"Hello agents" Will Hillard said as he held out his hand to shake theirs. "What brings you here?" he asked. Collins could tell that Mr. Hillard was in better spirits than the last time they saw him and wondered what had happened.

"Hello Mr. Hillard. We just wanted to stop by to see if you had remembered any information that might be useful to our investigation. We haven't been able to identify a suspect yet and thought maybe you may have remembered something. Anything no matter how small could be significant."

"I'm sorry, but I can't think of anyone who would do such terrible things. It was very difficult on my wife dealing with the guilt that our lottery may be the cause of our friend's deaths. But with the help of our other friends, we are trying to move on. We've cancelled the lottery in the hopes that no one else would get hurt. Our friends have been a great strength to us, and we are grateful that they want us to remain a part of their lives." Townsend could see a totally different man than when they last talked.

"We're glad that things are getting better for you and your wife. Since the lottery has been cancelled, I'm hopeful that the rest of your friends remain safe" Townsend said. "Rest assured that we will not stop until we catch the person who murdered your friends. In the meantime, if you think of anything, please give us a call." Townsend and Collins shook Mr. Hillard's hand then turned to leave. Townsend's gut was telling him that lottery or no lottery, this wasn't over.

The drive back to headquarters was driven in mostly silence. Both agents were mulling over the information that Mr. Hillard had provided and each coming up with the same conclusion. Collins broke the silence.

"I have a feeling that if the lottery was the reason for the deaths of four people, do they really think the murders will stop just because the lottery was cancelled? I don't think so." Townsend looked over at Collins and nodded in agreement.

"I feel the same way. I have a strong feeling that Denise McNeely and Angie Snowden are behind this whole thing. Denise McNeely doesn't seem like the kind of person who quits before she reaches her goal. And Angie Snowden has already had four people killed. She's got nothing to lose now and a big paycheck to gain. There's big money in murder for hire and Angie Snowden has to be right in the thick of it all.

We need to up the surveillance on Snowden. McNeely's not going to get her hands dirty, so it's Snowden ordering the hits. We've got to find this John Franklin character before anyone else get hurt." Collins agreed. Back at headquarters, Townsend briefed his team and assigned tasks accordingly.

The plan was to increase the surveillance on Snowden, but they had to be extra cautious. What they wanted was for her to think that she was off the hook and would drop her guard. They didn't know if she would order another hit, but they couldn't take the chance.

CHAPTER THIRTY

Angie didn't like the idea of taking out an-other one of the Hillard's friends, but it was the only way to get back on course. Denise wasn't going to wait forever. Angie had mulled over what to do next. She knew a hit had to be on one of the remaining lottery contenders. That would be the only way for the Hillard's to believe that they were at fault. It would likely send them over the edge and push them to sell the property.

After talking to David Flaherty, she knew that they were very close to getting rid of the property and moving away. Their guilt over the loss of four of their friends was unbearable. But then the damn group had to go and resurrect the Hillard's from their guilt pit and screw up the strides she had made.

The remaining friends were David Flaherty, but she would not hurt him. She was falling in love with him. There was Angie and Sean Callen and Frank and Phyllis Barber. She didn't know either couple, but David knew them well. She would need to gather some information on them in order to decide on who needed to go.

David was coming over for dinner that evening which would give her the perfect time to gather some useful information. After dinner and a few drinks, she would casually bring their names up. Her concern for his and their well-being after such a tragic loss would compel him to open up to her.

David arrived at Angie's house promptly at 7pm. She dressed in a low-cut red dress that enhanced her figure and turned heads whenever she wore it. It only needed to turn one head tonight. Music was playing in the background as she opened the door to let David in. He had brought a bottle of wine that he held up for her approval. She took his face in her hands and kissed him passionately, showing her approval.

As they entered the kitchen, David opened the wine and poured two glasses. Dinner was warming in the oven. The wine was a Merlot that had just a hint of fruitiness. He knew exactly what she liked and treated her like a queen. Any woman would be lucky to have him. She almost felt a tinge of guilt for using him to get information, but she blew it off telling herself that she really did care about him and the information he could provide was just a bonus.

They finished the first bottle of wine and opened a second to have during dinner. They ate dinner by candlelight. The mood was sensuous, and the wine was beginning to loosen David up. After they finished eating, they moved to the living room sofa. Before things heated up, she knew she needed to inquire about the Barbers and the Callen's.

"I'm so glad you came over tonight David" she said. "How are your friends holding up. I know you said that the Hillard's are doing good since you all went over there. I've never really met any of them, but I'd like to meet them. Anyone who is such a dear friend to you is someone that I would like to know also. Can you tell me a little about them? If I ever get to meet them, I'd like to know something about them." She watched his expression. He smiled at her request and told her that he wanted her to meet them, as well. He put his arm around her and spilled his guts. He told them about Sean and Angie Callen who were around his age. He talked about what they did for a living and how they got to know each other. He told her about the Barber's, who were about ten years older than he, but were a lot of fun to be around.

By the time he was done talking, she knew all she needed to know to set her next plan in motion. She turned to him and kissed him long and deep. Their passion grew and before they knew it, they were talking off each other's clothes and making their way to the bedroom. He satisfied her in more ways than he was aware. She would make it up to him some day when this whole deal was done, and a huge payday was hers.

David spent the night with Angie and when they woke up the next morning, they made love again. She was falling hard for David and knew he was falling for her. She could see no downside. Life was good right now and soon would be much better. All she wanted was to be able to share it with David; for them to have a future together. She wouldn't allow anything to get in the way.

CHAPTER THIRTY-ONE

The surveillance team had been sitting on Angie Snowden's house when they saw David Flaherty arrive at 7pm. They could see Angie answer the door and kiss David. They knew that David had been one of the lottery contenders and were concerned for his safety. Townsend told them to stay put, that Angie wouldn't do anything to hurt David in her own home. She was smarter than that. The fact that Angie had developed a relationship with David Flaherty was very interesting.

At 6am, the surveillance team was replaced with another team who were brought up to speed on the events of the evening. Around 9am, they saw David Flaherty leave Angie Snowden's house. Townsend had been right that she hadn't done anything to hurt him. In fact, they figured it was just the opposite by the smile on his face when he left.

Another team was tasked with looking into David Flaherty. They didn't think he was involved in any way, but they had to be sure. He did have something to gain when four of the lottery members were eliminated. He was one of the remaining five.

At a little past 9am, Angie Snowden got in her car and pulled out of her driveway. They waited for her to get far enough ahead, then pulled out to follow her. They had to be careful so not to be spotted. In order to remain discreet, a different team picked up the tail after about four blocks. They would continue this pattern in order to remain undetected.

About a mile from Snowden's house, she pulled into a strip mall and parked near an electronics store. The first surveillance team pulled into the strip mall and parked several spots away. They saw her enter the store but was unsure what she purchased when she exited the store ten minutes later.

The second surveillance team picked up the tail as she left the strip mall. Once she was back on the road, the agents from the first surveillance team went inside the electronics store to talk to the clerk. Showing their badges to the clerk, they asked what the woman that just left had purchased. The clerk told them she had purchased a burner phone and that she had been there before several weeks prior and purchased one then also.

It was a requirement of the store to maintain records of the serial numbers of the burner phones along with the name of the person who purchased them. Within minutes, the agents had the serial number and phone number of the burner phone that Angie Snowden just purchased. They were ecstatic.

The second surveillance team was told to continue to tail her while the first team went back to headquarters with the cell phone information. It looked like they might finally have caught a break.

Townsend and Collins were waiting when the agents arrived with the cell phone data. Immediate they got a warrant to track the calls made from the burner phone. There was only one reason why Snowden would purchase two separate burner phones. They were hoping that she would use it to contact John Franklin.

It was a waiting game now. Twenty-four hours after purchasing the phone, she still hadn't made a call. They were wondering if they had gotten excited for nothing. The surveillance team had said that Snowden had stopped at a grocery store and then went home. She had remained at her house up to the point of their update.

Townsend was getting antsy when finally, they got a notification that the phone was in use. The call only lasted a couple minutes, but they were able to obtain the number that Angie had called. After tracing the number, it was traced back to another burner phone. They knew it had to be John Franklin on the other end.

Although they couldn't listen to the conversation, they had the location of the cell tower that it pinged off of. Agents raced to the area but were unable to locate John Franklin. The fact that Snowden had made the call told agents that she was putting him to play.

Surveillance was ordered for the Callens and Barbers as well as the Hillard's. They had no idea who the target was, but they were sure that they all were in danger. They teetered on the idea of bringing them into protective custody, but they didn't want to tip their hand or cause a panic among the group. They had a vague description of John Franklin and would be able to step in before he could do any harm. At least, that was their intent.

CHAPTER THIRTY-TWO

Angie had called John Franklin to let him know his services would be needed once more. The conversation was brief, and she didn't give him any details but would be in touch with all the information he would need to carry out the hit. There was no hesitation in his voice, and she liked that. However, when everything was said and done, she wondered if she would need to eliminate him as a loose end.

So far, he had pulled off the hits flawlessly. The Feds had no idea who he was or that she was involved. His alias would never lead to his real identity nor would it lead to her. As long as the Feds couldn't track him down, he wouldn't need to be eliminated. Besides, she may need his services again in the future.

She had made the decision to put the hit on the Callens. They owned a small convenient store where they worked together occasionally. The hit could be made to look like a robbery gone bad. That would make it difficult to solve but she knew the Hillard's would lose two more friends and know that it couldn't have been a coincidence.

She needed to do a bit of reconnaissance herself to see if there were any cameras that could capture John's face. If there were, the hit might need to be done elsewhere. She would wait to see what she could find out before she made the decision and informed John.

The next morning, Angie drove the ten miles from her house to the convenient store owned by Sean and Angie Callen. It was on a side street with not a lot of traffic; a good sign. She was completely unaware that she was being followed. The agents passed up the store and drove a block, turned around and found a parking spot on the street where they could observe Angie. She sat in her car for a couple minutes before exiting. They noticed that she looked around the parking lot, which was strange, before she went inside.

Ten minutes later, she exited the store with only a soda in her hand. It seemed like a long time just to purchase a soda. The agents noted the name of the store and the time and details surrounding Snowden's visit.

Back on the road, they noticed that Angie took a different route. Instead of heading back the way she came, they followed her about three miles which took her over the Intercoastal bridge where she turned off to the left. They followed her onto River Road. The agents notified the rest of the team of Snowden's whereabouts to keep an eye out in case she was making a move.

But all she did was pull up to the gate of the Banana Bay Beach Resort community then turn around. From there, they followed her back to her house. It seemed awfully odd, so Townsend did a little research. They found out that the Callen's owned the convenient store that Snowden had visited, and already knew that the Callen's lived in the Banana Bay Beach community. It was the same community where the other four murdered friends lived.

"If I didn't know better, I'd say Angie Snowden just cased the Callen's business and their route from the store to their home. I'm willing to bet that the Callen's are her next target." Townsend said to the team. They were at odds whether to inform the Callen's or not. If they did, it could tip off Snowden and Franklin. This might be their only chance to catch them. They had no evidence linking any of the murders to Snowden and they still didn't have an ID on Franklin. They would need to beef up the protection on the Callen's without them knowing it. They couldn't allow anything to happen to them.

CHAPTER THIRTY-THREE

Denise McNeely sat in her office contemplating the latest developments in the Hillard property. It was devastating news that Angie Snowden had informed her of. She couldn't just sit back and wait for Angie to resolve the problem. She needed to talk to the Hillard's herself and pitch her proposal to them again.

Maybe they needed a little reminder that their friends were dropping like flies and that they should get out while they could. She would entice them with her generous offer hoping that they would bite. Mr. Hillard was a stubborn old man, but he had a soft spot where his wife was concerned.

She needed to remind him of her delicate state of mind and stress to him how he needed to get her away from all the sorrow that had been inflicted upon her in the past weeks. That would be the only way to convince him to sell. Offering them a handsome price for their property might show him that she was concerned for his wife's welfare and thus choosing her to sell the property to.

If the old codger wouldn't budge, she still had Angie planning on upping the ante. Things would start to move in her direction. All they needed was a little nudge. She didn't want to call the Hillard's and set up a meeting. She knew they would not agree to that. Catching them off-guard was what she needed to do. Just show up before they have time to discuss the matter.

She grabbed her purse and briefcase and headed over to the Hillard's. Denise had been working from home since it was a weekend. Her husband Bruce was out working in the yard when she yelled out that she had a to go on a sales call. He nodded and waved bye.

Denise's husband kept out of her real estate business. He left that up to her. His own business kept him busy enough. He had no idea the extremes his wife was willing to go to in order to close a deal. Denise often wondered how Bruce would handle some of the things she had done to promote her career. She did know that the steps she had taken to ensure the purchase of the Hillard place would not sit well with him. She had stepped over a line that would never allow her to reveal the real truth behind her attempt to persuade the Hillard's to sell.

But everything seemed to be under control. Even though she had been questioned by the Feds, she knew they couldn't find anything to lead back to her. If push came to shove, she would throw Angie under the bus. Never would she allow her reputation to be tarnished nor would she go to jail for what Angie had done.

It took about ten minutes to drive to the Hillard's. She knocked on the door and a few moments later, the door opened. A frown immediately spread across Will Hillard's face when he saw who was standing in front of him.

"Hello Mr. Hillard, I don't know if you remember me or not. I'm Denise McNeely with McNeely Real Estate Development. I spoke to you a few weeks ago regarding the sale of your house. I know you told me at the time that you weren't interested in selling, however, with everything that has happened over the last few weeks, I thought you might have reconsidered."

"I haven't" was his response.

"I understand that it hasn't been that long since the murders in the community, and I know that many of your neighbors are fearful for their safety. You should be too. I just wanted to re-state my offer to purchase your property. The sum I am willing to pay far exceeds the actual value of the place and the fact that some of the real estate values in the area could decline due to the recent murders, you might want to think about getting out while you can." She was surprised that she got her whole statement out before he stopped her, but he didn't say a word or slam the door in her face.

"I know that your wife suffered tremendously when your friends were killed. I can't imagine how hard it is to remain here knowing everything that has happened. I'm just trying to give you a way to get out from all the horror of the last few weeks and begin somewhere else." That last remark seemed to hit a nerve.

"Look Ms. McNeely, I appreciate your offer and at one point my wife and I had contemplated selling. But currently we have had a change of heart and have decided to remain here. We have good friends whose support has been a Godsend. So, at this current time, we are not interested in selling." Although it was not the exact words Denise wanted to hear, she did hear him say that they had considered selling. So, the murders did have an effect. All they needed was another bit a bad luck. That would surely push them over the edge.

She thanked Mr. Hillard for his time and turned to leave. She handed him her card.

"Just in case you ever decide to sell, my offer stands. Thanks again for your time." As she walked to her car, a smile crossed her face. They were close. If it hadn't been for the other friends that Angie had told her about who convinced them to stay, the sale would be in the books by now.

She needed Angie to put a rush on the next step. They had to hit while the iron was hot. The

Hillard's couldn't withstand another terrible blow. They would come running to her wanting to sell. She could feel it. She'd put a call into Angie to tell her to get it done. She didn't care what it was, it just needed to be done soon.

She swung by her office before heading home in order to contact Angie. She had to stress to Angie the need to work quickly. Angie would get the job done; she was sure of that much.

CHAPTER THIRTY-FOUR

B ack at the Hillard's, Will wasn't sure he should tell his wife about the visit from Denise McNeely. But not telling her wasn't an option. He walked into the kitchen and watched his wife pouring a glass of iced-tea and hand it to him.

"Was that the real estate lady who had come by here a few weeks ago Will?" Will took a sip of tea and knew he would need to tell her the reason for the visit.

"Yes, she stopped by to say that her offer to purchase the property was still on the table. She said that property values could decline because of what happened to our friends. I told her that we still were not interested in selling." He saw the frown on her face when he mentioned that property values could decline. It would be another blow to their friends. They all had houses in the community. She thought all the damage had been done, but it looked like they would suffer even more at their hands.

"Look Sally, our friends are great people.

They have forgiven us for anything we may have caused by creating that stupid lottery. I think they will be just as supportive. Besides, property values only matter if you're wanting to sell. None of our friends have said anything about selling. They'll be fine."

"If you say so Will. I couldn't bear another tragedy." He gave his wife a hug to reassure her that he was correct. After that, they headed out to the back to prepare for that evening's festivities. David Flaherty was bringing a date to the party that evening. It had been quite a while since David had dated anyone. They were happy to see him interested in someone again. They were looking forward to meeting Angie Snowden. The Callen's and Barbers were looking forward to meeting David's new fling as well.

Townsend and Collins had been updated on the surveillance on Angie Snowden. Nothing out of the ordinary had happened but they would remain in place. Townsend knew that something was in the works and they had to be vigilant.

There hadn't been any activity on John Franklin's phone either. It had been turned off immediately after the call from Angie Snowden. They may have another means of communication other than the burner phones, but they didn't know what it was. They knew Angie would have to contact him again once her plan was hammered out. She was doing the leg work before passing the plan on to Franklin.

Angie Snowden was the mastermind behind the actual murder plots, and Franklin was the one who carried it out. They had to find him. And Denise McNeely was the one funding it all. They were a deadly trio.

Townsend and Collins were having dinner at Cobalt restaurant when they received a call from the surveillance team assigned to Snowden. They reported that David Flaherty had picked up Snowden at 6pm. From there, they followed them to the Hillard residence.

While watching Flaherty and Snowden pull into the Hillard's driveway, they were followed shortly by the Callen's and then the Barber's. It looked as though there was going to be a party at the Hillard house.

Townsend didn't like the fact that Angie Snowden was in such close proximity to the Callen's. But after talking it over with Agent Collins, they were both in agreement that Angie Snowden would not be the one who did the dirty work, and it surely wouldn't be done with a group of potential witnesses there. They were sure that the Callen's would be ok, but there would need to be a tail on the Callen's when they left. That would be when they were most vulnerable.

The team that had been surveilling the Barber's had been reassigned to assist with the

Callen surveillance. It was Townsend's assumption that the target was Sean and Angie Callen. There was nothing that lead them to think that the Barbers were in danger any longer. There would be around the clock surveillance on the Callen's as well as Snowden. Whatever was going to go down, it was going to happen in the next few days.

The party went on for hours. They had surveillance on the waterway that had a direct view of the beach access from the Hillard place. Everyone was in ear contact and reported everything that was happening.

They observed Angie Snowden mingling with everyone and realized how cold a person had to be to know you had their friends killed and yet you could interact with them without a conscience. It sent a shiver up your spine knowing that people like that existed. They had to make sure they put Angie Snowden and the rest of the deadly trio behind bars forever.

The agents on the water later observed the group boarding the Hillard's boat and followed closely behind as the vessel made its way down the intercoastal waterway to a point where they had watched the sunset. It was as they had always done in the past. Nothing seemed to be amiss.

Angie Snowden sat back with David and enjoyed the ride. She could see why David had wanted this to continue. She could see herself as part of it too. But that would never be the case. This would likely be the last sunset cruise the group ever took together. In a way, she was sad that it had to end. But she could recreate this same scenario in another place once the job was done.

There was a sense of relief to the agents that nothing was going to go down that night. But it didn't ease the fear that there was still something in the works. When the Hillard's boat made its way back to their home, they all disembarked and soon everyone was ready to leave.

They were still unsure that the hit wouldn't be made on the way back to the Callen's, but agents were there to make sure nothing would go down. The Barber's left in their car followed by David Flaherty and Angie Snowden. Soon after, Angie and Sean Callen made their way to their car and left.

The agents kept a close tail on the Callen's to make sure that nothing went awry on their way back home. It was a tense situation for a while, but nothing seemed to be out of the ordinary. The Callen's drove home without any issues and entered their home. The agents stayed on site and surveilled their premises to make sure nothing happened. There was no activity was the report given to Townsend.

It was clear that the hit on the Callen's was

not in play that evening. But that didn't mean that it wasn't in the works. The Callen's lived in a gated community which allowed limited access to their home. It was more likely that the hit would take place either at their place of business or on their way home. They might need to bring the Callen's in on their assumptions. That way they could control the situation.

It was agreed that they would read in the Callen's on their thinking as to what they believed was going to happen.

Early the next morning, Townsend and Collins went to the Callen residence. They didn't know if they were being watched by Angie's hit man, but they had to bring the Callen's into the loop. They knocked on the door. Angie answered and recognized the agent. She was surprised to see them, but invited them in.

"Hello detectives. I'm surprised to see you" she said opening the door for then to enter. Townsend was the first to respond.

"Can you get your husband to join us? We need to talk to you about a current development."

Angie had a puzzled look on her face but called her husband from the kitchen to join them.

CHAPTER THIRTY-FIVE

The team that had been assigned to watch Angie Snowden had followed her and David Flaherty back to his place. Although it was a gated community, they were given the access code from the management under the guise that they were staking out a property across the inter-coastal and that Banana Bay gave them the necessary vantage point to carry out their operation.

The management was happy to oblige and were advised not to mention their presence to anyone in the community. It was agreed. From the parking area, they could keep constant watch on the front of the Flaherty residence.

The couple seemed very enamored with one another as they entered the residence. It was clear that Angie Snowden would not be leaving that evening. She had been picked up by Flaherty earlier and the two looked as though they had more private plans for the rest of the evening.

They watched as lights turned on in the home and movement could be seen through the open blinds. After a couple hours passed, they saw the lights on the lower level turn off just as a second-floor light came on. It looked as though the couple were taking the party to the bedroom.

The agents seated in the surveillance car looked at each other with a look that said it was going to be a long night. And just as expected, it was. But early the next morning, the agents saw Angie step out onto the beach area alone. They assumed she went out to take a smoke, however, when she pulled her phone out of her pocket, they alerted headquarters.

Just as they had thought, Angie was placing a call to John Franklin. The call lasted only ten seconds and then the connection was lost. It was apparent that she was setting up a meeting since she didn't have time to give any details over the phone. Ten seconds was enough time to name a place and time to meet and that was about all.

A few moments later, David Flaherty came out with two cups of coffee and joined her. They sat down together and sipped their coffee. The FBI team had no idea when or where the meeting was to take place; only that there was going to be a meeting.

Snowden and Flaherty sipped coffee for about thirty minutes before going back inside. Their conversation couldn't be heard unfortunately, but shortly after going inside, the two came back out and headed for Flaherty's car.

It was clear he was taking her home. If she had a meeting set up with Franklin, it was unlikely that the two were going out for breakfast.

Everyone was put on high alert. They had to track every move that Snowden made. They could not lose her at any cost.

Townsend and Collins had gone to the Callen residence at the same time that Snowden was at Flaherty's place. They only lived over one street and had to take extra precaution not to be noticed by Snowden. During the hour they met with Sean and Angie Callen, they informed them of the potential danger they could be in.

Fear had immediately rose in Angie Callen's face, but they reassured the couple that they would not be in any danger. They explained their plan to substitute agents who were similar in appearance to them to take their place at the store. It pained Townsend to have to inform them that the recent nightmare that they had been dealing with wasn't over yet

Sean Callen was reluctant to agree to their plan, but after explaining the danger involved in not cooperating, he backed down and agreed to do as they asked.

The plan was fairly simple, they were told. They would carry out their normal daily routines. They would be closely watched at all times. The two look-alike agents would be stationed in the store. They told the Callen's that they believed that the attempt on them would likely take place once they left the store for the evening and were on their way home.

When it was time to close up shop, instead of Angie and Sean getting into their car, they would be replaced by the two agents who would be dressed in the same attire. The agents would be the ones driving the Callen's car. If an attempt was made on them during the drive, they would be ready to apprehend their suspect.

When Townsend and Collins were ready to leave, they reassured the Callen's that this would soon be over and the person who killed their friends would pay for what they did. They could see that the Callen's were nervous, and they could understand why. But they would protect them. They stressed to the Callen's that they were to tell no one about what was going on. No friends, no relatives, no one. Sean and Angie both agreed.

Before leaving the Callen residence, Townsend had cleared it with the other agents that Snowden and Flaherty had left the area. They were able to leave undetected. Now the ball was in Snowden's court. They were sure that she would be meeting with Franklin to set the plan in motion.

A team of six agents in three cars were following David Flaherty's car with extreme caution not to be noticed. Angie Snowden was dropped off at her house. Flaherty bent over and kissed her but did not exit the car. Angie went inside her home and Flaherty drove off. All three cars had Snowden's house covered so she couldn't leave without being seen.

They were sure she hadn't noticed them since they were experts at tailing a suspect without be spotted. That was the reason for three cars. Each one would follow for a certain distance, then turn off. The next car would pick up the tail. That would go on for as long as it took.

Now, all three cars were in place and stationery until Snowden made her move.

Thirty minutes later, Angie's garage door opened, and her black Mercedes backed out onto the street. It was visually verified that it was Angie driving. Once she was on the road, the first car slipped in about a block behind. It was crucial that they not lose her. She headed north toward Route 98 which was a main road out of Pensacola which allowed the surveillance team to put a little further distance between them. They could see the black Mercedes about a quarter mile ahead.

The Mercedes followed Route 98 for several miles. She crossed the bridge over Pensacola Bay into Lillian. They had no idea if she was taking them on a wild goose chase or was being overly cautious.

They knew she couldn't have spotted them,

so they decided that she was being overly cautious. She headed down Route 98 all the way to Route 59 where she turned left. When she turned left into the Tanger Outlet Mall, they wondered if she was going shopping. But they realized that by going to the mall, she would be much harder to surveil.

All three cars had entered the mall and zigzagged around to look like random customers looking for parking. Up ahead, they saw the black Mercedes pull into a parking spot where Snowden immediately got out of her car. She quickly went through a walkway that went through a curved alcove to the other side of the mall which had many other stores. By the time the agents could get to the other side, Snowden had already ducked into one of the stores.

"Damnit, the female agent said. Where'd she go?"

"She had to go into one of these stores nearby. She didn't have time to get further away" said her partner. The other four agents caught up. They could see that they had lost her but knew she had to be in one of the stores. They would spread out and go into each store to see if they could find her. They desperately needed an ID on John Franklin.

As they entered each of the stores, they could not find Angie Snowden or anyone they thought might be John Franklin. After searching for an hour and covering all the stores she could have possibly entered, they met back up at the walk-way where they had lost her.

They walked back through to the parking lot where they left their cars.

"Shit, the Mercedes is gone" the female agent said. Her partner spoke up.

"There was no way she could have gotten past us." Then it hit them. She had to know that she was being watched and had purposely led them to the mall. They knew she had worked at the mall a few years before. She obviously used that knowledge and went into the store then ex-ited out the rear door, got in her car and left. She could be anywhere by now.

No one wanted to make the call to Townsend to inform him that they had lost Angie Snowden and that she was probably meeting up with Franklin as they spoke. Once the call was made, Townsend nearly broke the phone when he slammed it down. They quickly put out a bolo on the black Mercedes, but knew by the time they found it, her meeting would be over. There was no doubt that they were dealing with a professional.

They had underestimated Angie Snowden, but that would not happen again. Even though they had no ID on John Franklin or what kind of vehicle he drove, they still had a plan in place. It would just be harder to know when and where he would strike. His substitute agents would be in danger, but they were professionals as well. Townsend was confident that they would still catch John Franklin in the act. Once he was in custody, they would get him to flip on Angie Snowden and she would flip on Denise McNeely. They would try and save themselves because that's what criminals do.

CHAPTER THIRTY-SIX

Townsend was irate when he heard the news that his agents had lost the tail on Snowden. They needed to know what Franklin was driving. Not knowing was a glitch they couldn't afford. But they had to deal with what they had. The plan with the Callen's would require more manpower, but that wasn't an issue. They could assign as many agents as needed, but they were fairly sure that Snowden knew that she was being watched. She would have passed that information on to Franklin, who would need to take extra caution.

They also knew that Franklin had pulled off four murders without leaving a trace. He was good at what he did, and they could not take that for granted. The Callen's were to relieve their daytime clerk at 6pm. The swap agents would be at the store before the Callen's were scheduled to arrive. A back office would provide cover for the agents while the Callen's manned the store.

Angie and Sean drove to the store with agents following to ensure no attempt was made on the drive to the store. Everything seemed normal on the drive to the store. The Callen's parked in their usual spot and entered the store. The cashier and stocker had left by 6:30. The evening progressed without incident.

Occasionally, Sean or Angie would enter the office to update the agents who had been watching the activity in the store on the cameras that were in place in several areas within the store. Several customers had come and gone without any suspicious activity. The store closed at 11pm and when that time was near, Sean went and locked the front door while they tallied up the receipts for the day and took the money to the office. That was when the switch took place.

Instead of Angie and Sean leaving the premises through the front door, the swap agents, who were dressed identical to the Callen's came to the front of the store, no one could tell it wasn't Angie and Sean. The agents unlocked the front door, exited the store, then got into the Callen's car and pulled out of the parking lot.

The surveillance teams were in place to follow the Callen's car as they left the store and made their usual route back towards their house. Everyone was in communication with the agents as they drove the route that Snowden had previously scoped out. No one made an attempt to stop the Callen's vehicle nor did they see anything suspicious along the way.

The agent's pulled into the Callen's gated community without any problems. It was a disappointment to the team. It turned out that it was not the night that the attempt on the Callen's would take place. But they knew that an attempt would be made, and they would perform the same routine every night until Franklin made his move.

It was an inconvenience for the Callen's to have to remain in their store office for two hours after they closed the store before they were escorted out the back door and driven home. But they understood the precautions that needed to be made. Their lives were at stake and they wanted this to be over.

They followed the same routine for four days with no attempts from Franklin. They were beginning to think that the plan had been aborted. But on the fifth day, things changed. Townsend knew that Franklin had to be watching the store from somewhere that eluded them. But they knew that there was a job that needed to be done and Franklin had to be sure that he could pull it off without being detected.

Franklin had been watching the store from a vantage point that the agents were unaware of. But they were ready. Townsend made sure that the route that the agents took was the same every night. They knew that Franklin was too smart to follow them right from the parking lot.

But they had agents stationed at every point along the way.

About a half mile into the drive to the Callen residence, they noticed a black sedan pull out of a side street about a block after the agents in the Callen's car passed. The agents stayed back far enough to not be exposed, but informed other agents of the black sedan's location.

Along a dark stretch of road, the black sedan closed the distance between itself and the Callen's car. The agents in the Callen's car could see the black sedan approaching behind them. He was picking up speed and as the sedan was within a car's length, he veered around them and forced them off the road.

The agents didn't know what Franklin had in store as they were forced to pull over on the darkened shoulder of the road. Once the Callen's car was off the side of the road, the sedan pulled in front blocking their way. A man jumped from the car and ran to the Callen's car and pulled a gun. As he walked to the car assuming that Angie and Sean Callen were helpless, he raised his pistol. But before he could get a shot off, one of the agents fired at Franklin hitting him in the shoulder.

Franklin went down and both agents jumped from their car. Franklin's gun had been knocked away on the impact of the bullet to his shoulder. They quickly apprehended him and cuffed him.

He cursed at them when he knew he had been set up. Thankfully, the agent's shot had been well placed so as not to kill Franklin. He knew he was caught, but he had no idea what they had on him.

Franklin was taken into custody where he was met by Townsend and Collins. They had Franklin on attempted murder to start with. Once they had Franklin fingerprinted, they had his real identity. His real name was Ray Ramey. He had a rap sheet that was extensive, but he had never been convicted of anything. He likely had friends in high places who made sure he wouldn't spend much time in prison.

Townsend and Collins had him in the interrogation room and questioned him on why he would want to kill Angie and Sean Callen. He quickly asked for an attorney, so the questioning had to stop. They let him sit in the interrogation room until his attorney showed up. Once his attorney was present, they joined them in the interrogation room and told the attorney what they had on his client. They also said that they would be willing to work out a deal if Ramey would give up Angie Snowden.

He was reluctant to talk, and his attorney said that they needed time to discuss his options. Townsend was confident that Ramey would do whatever it took to save himself, but for the time being, they would keep him in custody.

The news media had already caught wind

of the arrest and it was aired on the news before Townsend could squelch it. Angie Snowden knew that the hit had been thwarted and feared that her guy would squeal. She had to put a stop to it.

Angie had connections that reached far into the law enforcement realms and knew she had to do something to keep Ray Ramey from fingering her. But she couldn't get to him soon enough.

Ramey made a deal to tell the FBI who had hired him and had made a statement to Townsend saying as much. After Ramey had said who had paid him to kill all four victims, he was placed in a cell without bail. The next morning, an official deal was to be printed up for Ramey to sign. Townsend finally had the goods on Angie Snowden. She, in turn, would turn on Denise McNeely to save herself some jail time.

The next morning as Townsend and Collins were driving to the police station where Ramey was being held, Townsend's phone rang. As he listened to the voice on the other end, Collins could tell the news was not good. When Townsend ended the call, he slammed his fist into the dash. He had just received word that Ray Ramey had been found dead in his cell. He had been poisoned.

It was a major blow to their case since they hadn't gotten the written statement from

Ramey. Now they had no way to link the murders to Snowden or McNeely.

Somehow, Snowden had gotten to Ramey. She had connections deeper than they knew and had had Ramey killed while he was in his cell. It was not over yet.

CHAPTER THIRTY-SEVEN

News broke the next morning of the arrest of Ray Ramey and his connections to the homicides of four local residents of the Banana Bay Community. Relief swept through the small community knowing that the killer of their friends had not only been caught but had also been murdered in his cell. To them, it was finally over.

But to Townsend, Collins and the FBI team, they knew that it wasn't over yet. The real culprits were still at large, and their only witness was now dead.

Angie watched the news story air on television. She knew she was almost in the clear since the FBI couldn't prove her involvement in the crimes. There was only one loose end who could pin the murders on her. Denise McNeely knew what Angie had done to help her in getting the Hillard's to sell.

Denise McNeely would flip on her in a heartbeat. She couldn't let that happen. She called Denise and said she needed to talk to her. Denise had watched the news as well and was skeptical about meeting Angie. But she knew she had to reassure her that she would never divulge any of their involvement in the murders.

Angie told Denise that she needed to talk to her so they could get their stories straight. If they played their cards right, nothing would lead back to either of them. What Angie didn't know was that the FBI had already contacted McNeely and told her what they knew had gone down and that she was involved.

They offered McNeely a deal that if she got Angie to talk about the hits she had ordered, that she would be offered leniency on the charges that they could put on her. Denise McNeely, wanting to save her own ass, had agreed.

Denise had agreed to wear a wire and meet with Angie to get her to admit to her role in hiring Ramey to carry out the hits on the lottery recipients in return for immunity. Denise had been shrewd in her negotiations with the Feds. They had no proof unless she got Angie on tape. Therefore, they had to offer total immunity.

Denise had told Townsend that she had enlisted the help of Angie Snowden to get the Hillard's to sell their property but had no idea that she would resort to murder to make it happen.

McNeely told Townsend that she did not tell Angie to murder anyone. Angie had taken that aspect of the deal on her own and had hired Ramey to carry out the murders. McNeely said that when she heard of the murders of the Banana Bay residents, she confronted Snowden who had said that she would do whatever it took to get the job done.

They believed McNeely when she said that she had never asked Angie Snowden to do the things she had done but thought she knew about the murders. She was willing to do whatever it took to clear her name.

They told McNeely to set up a meeting like Snowden had asked and to wear a wire so they could nail Snowden for ordering the hits. Denise said she would.

Denise contacted Angie Snowden to arrange a time to meet. She told Angie that she was concerned that the FBI would link Ramey to her and that they needed to come up with a plan. Angie told Denise to meet her in a parking garage as soon as possible. They agreed to meet at a parking garage in Orange Beach called Escapes to the Shores. Angie knew that it was a covered parking garage where there was plenty of privacy.

Denise agreed to meet her there that evening at 10pm. They were to meet on the second level. They could have a discussion there to decide what their story would be. Denise had been wired up and was told to get Angie to disclose what she had done so they could develop a story that would keep them in the clear.

Agents were sent to the meeting place an hour ahead of time so they could apprehend Snowden once they had her confession on tape. Denise was advised to arrive at the location thirty minutes before the meeting time so the agents could be in place.

At 9:30pm, Denise arrived at the Escapes to the Shores parking garage and parked on the second level. She waited until she saw Snowden's car pull onto the second level and park across from Denise's car. The two women exited their cars. Denise walked over to Angie's car.

"So, what's the plan Angie? I'm pretty freaked out about this whole thing."

"Don't worry Denise, they will never get you to admit to anything" Angie said as she pulled out a nine-millimeter handgun and shot Denise in the head. Denise dropped to the ground just as agents jumped from their cars and yelled for Angie to drop the gun.

Angie turned towards the approaching agents and pointed her gun at them. A barrage of bullets rang out hitting Angie Snowden several times. Angie Snowden fell to the ground in a pool of blood next to Denise McNeely. Both were pronounced dead at the scene.

No one expected it to go down like that. The agents on the scene had checked both women for a pulse, but both were dead. It wasn't how the FBI wanted it to go down, but in the end, all three suspects that had conspired to kill people in the hopes of greater wealth, were all dead. It was over.

Townsend and Collins had been on the scene when it all went down. They did not like the fact that three people were dead, but the three people that were dead had murdered, or had been responsible for the murders, and now were no longer breathing. The Hillard's and the people of the Banana Bay Beach community were no longer in danger. It was a sad ending to an even sadder series of events. It's just the way it turns out sometimes.

CHAPTER THIRTY-EIGHT

Breaking news splashed across every news outlet across the country that a major conspiracy to purchase a property which was hoped to end up in the construction of a luxury condominium complex near the Banana Bay Beach resort resulted in the deaths of four innocent people, and had ended in the deaths of the three people involved in the conspiracy.

It sent shock waves through the community especially to those that were closely related to the incident. Many rumors surfaced about the McNeely Real Estate Development which was so well known to the area. Those involved in the ordeal had suffered tremendous loss over the deaths of their friends who were innocent victims in the scheme.

The news outlets had tried to interview those closely affected by the ordeal but were not willing to speak of their trauma. It had devastated the small community but those involved had vowed to not let the unspeakable acts of some, devour the closeness of the family they had come to know.

The FBI had made statements regarding their efforts to find the perpetrators of the crimes to much dismay. They could only hope that those closely affected by the deeds of Denise McNeely, Angie Snowden and Ray Ramey could now move on knowing that their community was safe. They only wished that they could have captured those who had done such horrible crimes could have been apprehended sooner.

EPILOGUE

Time passes slowly after a tragedy. Time doesn't always heal all wounds.

Townsend and Collins had solved the crimes but, in their minds, not quickly enough. Being an FBI agent, a person sees many bad deeds. Some deeds go unpunished, and for that, a person must deal with the failure. Townsend and Collins moved on to other crimes that needed their attention.

For the Hillard's, it would take time to heal the scars of the murders of their friends. Guilt will always be a part of what happened to their dear friends. But the friends that remained, love and forgiveness would play a large part in the healing process.

True friendship never dies. Their lives are forever changed by the deeds of some very evil people. But they would remain true friends forever. No one can ever know if the kindness of someone would lead to evil deeds of another.

In the end, the Hillard's, along with Phyllis and Frank Barber, Sean and Angie Snowden and

David Flaherty would remain dear friends. Their lives would become richer for knowing their lost friends. The memories of those who are gone for no just reason, will live in their hearts forever.

It was devastating to David Flaherty knowing that the woman he was falling in love with could be so evil. He had not seen any signs. He doubted his judgement. But the group reassured him that they had all been fooled by Angie Snowden. He promised he would not punish himself over it. It wouldn't be easy, but he was willing to try.

The Hillard's continued their parties with their friends for many years to come. David Flaherty had gotten married two years after the ordeal and was living a happy life.

And as each sun set in the sky, they would toast their dear departed friends and know that they were there in spirit, happy that they would carry on the tradition.

As the sun set over the horizon, glasses were raised in their honor.

"Here's to Thomas, Ginger, Lyle, and Josh, you are always in our hearts."

Other books by Elizabeth Farris:

The Water's Edge – reviewed by Red City Review... *The Water's Edge* will suck you in and pull you under as Elizabeth Farris tells you a tale of abduction, torture and murder. Yet, there is a beautiful love story just beneath the surface of *The Water's Edge* as well. Elizabeth Farris' *The Water's Edge* may make you think twice about what really lies just under the surface.

Deadly Secrets

Fatal Alliance

The Bone Field

Final Betrayal

Shattered

CPSIA information can be obtained
at www.ICGtesting.com
Printed in the USA
FSHW022158180719
60153FS

9 781977 215574